The Laelynn
Part 1

Brett Winczura

CONTENTS

PROLOGUE

Inside the room, the walls moved with the flickering of the many candles lining the windowsill above the bed and stretching out along the shelves that wrapped around the room. They offered little heat against the bitterly cold room.

The smell of flowers was strong, filling every corner with their sweet odour. Hundreds of bouquets sat on the floor and crept their way up the walls, piled high on one another in the corners of the room. They were gifts to the saviour, Mr. Laelynn, from his loyal followers for the journey he was about to embark on.

The door to the room opened, causing the candles to waver back and forth. The shadows jumped as two men walked in and stood aside to allow Mr. Laelynn to enter. He looked around confidently, inspecting the room with his gaze.

"Everything is ready, Mr. Laelynn," one of the men said, gesturing to the waiting bed, which had its blankets neatly folded down about halfway.

He walked to it and sat down, removing his shoes and sliding them on the floor to the foot of the bed. He rested his hands on his knees and closed his eyes, slowing his breathing in anticipation.

One of the men walked towards a small table against the furthest wall and picked up a book, then handed it to Mr. Laelynn, stepping back as he grabbed it and set it beside him. It was a few inches thick and emblazoned on the front were two concentric circles. It was the book they all diligently followed.

He lay down, resting his head on the pillow and pulling the blankets up to his waist. He reached for the book and laid it on his chest.

One of the men set two pills in his hand, and then he put them in his mouth and bit down. The slight stinging sensation they caused soon faded.

"You may both leave," he said.

The men walked to the door and opened it quietly. As the first disappeared into the hallway, the second turned and looked at Mr. Laelynn. He nodded slightly and shut the door.

The sounds of his breathing became slower and slower, quieter and quieter, until the last exhale.

Undoubtedly, his return was already anticipated by the other cult members.

1

Inside the room, Reena sat on the couch and hung her head back, breathing deeply and sighing loudly. She knew she needed a break. Alan had been talking about a vacation within the next few weeks, and she felt as though it would be good timing.

As she waited for Dr. Carrie to come speak to her, she replayed the last few minutes in her mind. A father and his son had been run over a couple blocks from the hospital, and during the transport, the father had died. The son was in bad shape; his left leg was nearly severed at the knee, he had a large gash in his abdomen that was gushing blood, and a head wound that would require a lot of work to fix.

She became distracted while attending to the boy and knocked a large cart of supplies over. It crashed to the ground and she was told to leave the room by the doctor.

In her four years as a nurse at the trauma center, she had seen her share of accidents. It wasn't uncommon to have entire families on stretchers, bleeding profusely and screaming in pain. It was something she had grown accustomed to, but recently she was feeling burned out from a summer of car accidents, suicide attempts, and domestic abuse cases.

"We need to talk," Dr. Carrie said as he came rushing into the room, jarring her from the half-sleeping state she was in. "You need to be careful what you're doing in the trauma room," he said, throwing his hands in the air. "We need senior nurses to be present, all of the time."

She nodded. Staff rotation in the trauma area was high, and new nurses were always being hired. Staff burnout was rampant, and she knew she was bordering on the same feelings that plagued so many others.

"I know," she said timidly, knowing there was no use in making any excuses. "I'm sorry."

He sighed and walked towards the door. "I want you to consider taking a few weeks off work to pull yourself together. I know this job isn't easy, and I know you're tired, but we all need you to be the best you can."

She nodded. "I'll talk to Alan and let you know tomorrow."

He nodded and stepped through the door, shutting it behind him and leaving Reena in silence.

She leaned back, images floating through her mind. In the last week alone, she had two patients die while she was on shift; an elderly man who had suffered a heart attack and a girl in her early twenties who overdosed on fentanyl while with her friends. The man, his wife, and their grandchildren had been taking an early morning walk when he grabbed his chest and fell over. His wife ran to him as his grandkids watched from a distance. He was rushed to the hospital and died shortly after arriving. The girl and her friends had been getting high, smoking a joint that was unknowingly laced with crushed fentanyl. She had begun to seize and lost consciousness when the ambulance was called. Once at the hospital, she died. The others who smoked the joint were given Narcan and lived.

Reena walked into Hillstone, one of her favourite restaurants and scanned the room, searching for Alan. Their usual routine was to meet for dinner and then head home together.

He was an electrician, and they had met while both of them were at work. The hospital was having some electrical repairs done and he was working in the nurses' station for a few days. They exchanged numbers and slowly became close. Two years later, he proposed and they moved in together; buying a condo a year later in Sunnyside.

A scream escaped her lungs as Alan's hands came around her stomach and grabbed her. She spun around and he kissed her softly.

"How was your day?" he asked, leading the way to their table.

"It was tiring. We had a young kid come in who had been hit by a truck. His father died on the way to the hospital, and he's badly injured."

He nodded as he removed his coat and set it beside him on the chair. "How is he doing?"

She frowned. "Stable. I checked before I left for the day and things seemed to be improving slightly. He'll be down for a long time, though. I can't imagine how he'll feel when he's told his father didn't make it."

"That's out of your hands. You can't take all of the emotional responsibility onto yourself, Reena," he said, sliding his hands across the table and holding hers. He was all too familiar with her habit of over-empathizing with the patients she dealt with, and he knew how destructive it was to her.

"I know," she said, removing one hand from his grasp and taking a sip of her wine. "Dr. Carrie advised I take a few weeks off work to catch my breath."

He smiled and nodded his head, seemingly excited to hear the doctor's recommendation.

She rolled her eyes at him. "I agree with him, and you too. I was thinking about it today and I'm going to take a couple weeks off, starting next week," she said, taking another sip of wine.

He nodded. "I can take the same weeks off as you! I'm the boss!" he laughed. "Where should we go?".

"Go?" she asked. "I thought we could stay home and do those renovations we wanted to do."

"We don't need two weeks to do that," he said. "A week would be fine. Let's go somewhere for one week and stay home for another. It'll be great!"

She pondered the thought for a few moments and then smiled. "That's a good idea, but the second week will be manual labour, sweat, and lots of swearing."

He took a sip of his beer and shoved his menu aside. "It's settled then. A week away and a week at home."

Two hours after they had eaten and had enough alcohol, he pulled out his phone and turned it on.

"Let's book a holiday now!" he said, giggling as he opened the internet.

She laughed too, realizing that the thought of time away with him was something she really wanted.

After many searches online for travel deals, they had stumbled upon a resort along the Caribbean, in the state of Quintana Roo in Mexico. It was an older hotel from the nineteen thirties but had good reviews.

"It sounds nice, and it's more than affordable," she said, holding the edge of the phone as he scrolled through the pictures. "What's it called?"

"The Laelynn," he said. "Should I book it?"

She paused for a moment and thought. "Yes, do it now before I can say no."

"Alright," he said, pulling his wallet from his pocket and removing his credit card. He punched in the required information and waited.

"I didn't think your credit limit was that high" she said.

"It's my work card," he said, waiting for the transaction to complete.

"I'm marrying the right guy," she joked, sipping at her wine.

He smiled and finished up the transaction. "In nine days, we'll be in Mexico and enjoying some time to ourselves."

She smiled, too, and breathed a sigh of relief. She couldn't wait. "A toast?" she asked, raising her glass.

He smiled and raised his, lightly tapping them against one another.

2

The week before their vacation went by quickly. They spent their time packing and organizing their suitcases, researching the resorts activities, and arranging for friends to come by and check up on their condo.

"I'm so excited!" Alan kept saying.

"I know, you've already told me a hundred times," Reena would say, smiling.

"How many changes of clothes should I take?" he asked the evening before they were going to leave.

"However many you think you'll need. Why is it that the man of the house is having issues deciding on the right amount of clothing, and I, the wife, have finished my packing with the smallest amount of clothing needed for the week?" she said, gently slapping his back. She had grown accustomed to calling herself the wife, even though the wedding was just over a year away.

He laughed and grabbed her, spinning her around and slowly lowering her onto the bed. "You're the wife and I'm just the man of the house? I can't be the husband?" he said, nuzzling his face into her neck.

"You can be whatever you'd like to be," she said as she rubbed his back.

He breathed in slowly and rested the weight of his head against hers. "I'm so excited."

"I am too," she whispered. She glanced at the clock. It read ten thirty. "We should get ready for bed," she said. "We need to be up at five."

He pushed himself to the side and rolled over onto his back. "I don't think I'll be able to sleep. Will you?" he asked.

She wondered for a second and sighed. "Probably not, but let's try. We don't want to be tired or bitchy tomorrow."

The alarm beeped loudly, and both woke from their sleep with groggy eyes. They laid in bed for a few minutes before shuffling their feet to the floor.

"I'm going to shower," he said, removing his pajamas and dropping them into the laundry basket. "Do you want to come?"

She shook her head. "You go. I'm going to pack a couple more things and then tidy up a bit. I'll go when you're done."

He walked into the bathroom, his body bouncing off the door frame in his tired state. A few moments later the water turned on and steam slowly crept into the bedroom.

Reena spent the next twenty minutes making the bed, changing the garbage, unloading the dishwasher, and straightening the sofa cushions. She didn't like the idea of coming back to a messy home.

"All yours," Alan yelled as he came into the bedroom.

She pinched his ass as he was putting on his underwear. He jumped and laughed.

"I'll be right out," she said, shutting the bathroom door behind her.

Realizing he forgot to pack condoms, he reached towards his nightstand and pulled them out, putting them in the bottom of his suitcase. They had talked about kids for the future, but that wasn't a necessary commitment for them now, if ever.

He laid down on the bed and flipped through the travel books he'd bought. Highlighted on each page were the places they had agreed on seeing or things they agreed on doing. He liked the idea of hiking and swimming, while she liked the idea of relaxing on the beach with a glass of wine and reading some books. They would compromise.

Their hotel was just off the beach, nestled against a forest that stretched far inland. The pictures of it excited them.

"You're not sleeping, are you?" Reena asked as she came into the bedroom.

He shook his head and dropped the books into his suitcase, next to his laptop. "I was just looking at the things we planned to do."

She sat on the bed. "If we don't hurry, we'll be spending the next two weeks doing renovations," she said, leaning back and kissing him.

He jumped from the bed and ran to his waiting clothes, throwing them on. He grabbed his suitcases and zipped them closed, tossing them on the bed. "I'm ready, you're the one that's not," he said, smirking.

"Well then, since you're so quick, why don't you start loading all the bags and I'll finish getting ready," she replied as she pulled her pants up.

He sighed and began carrying them out. "Looks like the man of the house wins again," he yelled from the living room as he unlocked the front door.

She smiled, pulling her shirt over her bra and straightening her hair.

As the food cart on the plane stopped at their seats, they looked at it in anticipation. They had waited to eat breakfast until they arrived at the airport, but the ride from their condo took longer than they expected.

"I'm starving!" Reena said, taking the snack the stewardess handed to her. She felt disappointed. A small cinnamon bun with almost no icing.

"Why didn't we eat before we left the house?" Alan asked, holding his in the air.

She looked at the stewardess and smiled. "Can we get another one?"

The woman looked at her disapprovingly, shook her head, and firmly declined. "If we give everyone more than one, then someone won't get theirs," she said as she pushed the cart further up the aisle, disappearing beyond their sight.

"Let's hope the resort is nicer than that woman was," Alan mumbled, biting into his cinnamon bun.

"We can hope," she said, taking another bite of her bun.

He wiped his hands clean on a napkin and shoved it into his pocket. He pulled out one of the travel books he had put into his jacket and started flipping through the pages, reading out loud. He found a section at the back of the book regarding the hotel itself and paused, becoming quiet while he scanned the pages and read to himself.

"What did you find that's so interesting?" she asked, staring out the window at the blanket of white clouds and the countryside below them.

He cleared his throat. "It's a section on the history of the hotel. It was built by a man named Arthur Laelynn. It's been a family business for years; three generations of people have owned it."

She turned to him, feeling tired. "What else does it say?"

He continued reading a bit and then spoke. "It was the first resort built in the area, but there's another one now that's built a few miles from it that's called Sun Garden Resort."

She closed her eyes. "Keep reading and let me know what you find out."

He watched her slowly fall asleep. They had another two hours and forty-five minutes until they arrived in Cancun. He closed the book, set it beside him, and stood up. He opened his carry-on bag from the overhead compartment and slid out his laptop.

Sitting down, he turned it on and waited, looking behind him at the mix of passengers, mostly Spanish-speaking. Neither of them spoke Spanish and he thought they should learn some greetings.

When the laptop was ready, he opened the internet and clicked on the search bar. "*Laelynn Resort, Quintana Roo, Mexico,*" he typed and numerous pages showed up; the link to the hotels main website and many other pages. He clicked one and read silently.

"Attention," the pilot said through the speakers. "We'll soon be beginning out descent into Cancun, and we'd like to ask that you please put your trays up. Thank you."

"Hello, Sleeping Beauty," Alan said, continuing to look at the computer screen as Reena woke up.

She smiled. "What have you been doing?" she asked, stretching her arms.

"I've been researching the hotel," he said, closing the browser.

"And what did you find out?"

Before he could answer, the stewardess returned and tapped the computer. "Tray's up!" she said and walked away.

He looked at Reena. "Such a bitch," he said, shutting the laptop and flipping the tray up. "Apparently, it's a haunted hotel, if fan made websites can be trusted."

She laughed. "Can they ever?"

He raised his eyebrows. "Apparently there's been numerous missing person's cases linked to the hotel, and it's been continually reported that it's full of ghostly activity."

"Do you think we'll run into any ghost hunters?" she asked, feeling herself shudder at the idea of missing people.

He laughed. "It's also long been suspected of being the residence of a cult."

"Ghosts and cults," she said, rolling her eyes. "And here I thought we'd have a boring time hiking through a forest and swimming with sharks."

The plane began its descent as she looked out over the ocean. The crystal-blue water was as clear as the sky. She smiled and reached for Alan's hand, kissing the top of it.

The bus ride from Cancun to the resort was two hours.

A middle-aged man wearing a shirt designed with tropical trees leaned over and began talking to them. "Where are you two from?" he asked through a thick Texan accent.

Alan reached out and shook his hand. "My wife and I are from New York. We're here for a vacation."

The man reached to Reena and shook her hand as well. "I'm John, and this is my wife, Lily," he said, motioning towards the woman seated next to him.

"Hi," Lily said, shyly.

"I'm Alan, and this is Reena," Alan said, touching her back lightly.

"Do you have any children?" John asked.

Alan and Reena both gave a small laugh. "No, we're not sure we want any," Reena said, looking to Alan.

"We're not sure if we're the parenting type," he said.

At this, Lily seemed to gain her confidence. "Oh! You must! Children are what makes life matter!" she said, sliding herself to the edge of her seat.

John laughed and turned to her, then back to Alan and Reena.

"We have three kids already, and if I agreed, we'd be having three more!"

Alan and Reena shared a glance. People who got overly excited about kids were the types of people they liked to avoid.

"Maybe one day," Reena said.

"Where are your kids?" asked Alan.

Lily leaned forward. "They're back home. We decided to take a vacation by ourselves this time. It's been five years since we've done this!"

"Where are you two staying?" asked John.

"At the Laelynn," Alan said.

John smiled brightly. "Us too!" he said, shifting his body towards Lily.

Reena gave a slight groan under her breath, just loud enough for Alan to hear, and turned towards John. "That's great!" she said, trying to act as enthusiastic as she could.

During the rest of the bus ride, Alan and Reena got to know a bit more about John and Lily, while also trying to get a few minutes of sleep. It didn't work well, and just as Reena was about to tell them they'd chat more later on, the bus driver called out that they were approaching their first stop. The Laelynn.

A few passengers stood and ushered their way to the front as the bus driver opened the doors and got out. He opened the hatch, allowing the compartment door to slide up, and handed everyone their bags. Slowly the small crowd turned and walked towards the resort entrance. Metal gates, covered in intricate twisted strips of metal with vines threaded throughout, welcomed them.

As the bus pulled away, so did its shadow and the sun shone brightly. It blinded those who weren't expecting it, and everyone was silent for a moment as the sounds of distant waves reached their ears. They all turned and looked towards the sound; down the road lined with flowers and bushes, the ocean splashed in the distance, and the sun sparkled on the light blue surface.

The brown concrete walls of the resort were high and decorated with vines and colourful plants. On the top, there were metal spikes spaced every few inches, about a foot tall, that looked extremely sharp at the point; their dangerous appeal was softened by the bright greens and pinks that the flowers provided. The actual hotel wasn't visible from the road, but as they continued walking on the brick walkway, it slowly came into view.

3

Reena was cuddled up on the couch, a blanket protecting her from the cold that lingered in the room, and the TV flashed cartoons across the screen. The bills were far behind, and her mother and father didn't seem to care, even though the heat had been turned off. She was ten years old at the time, and it was a change from a year earlier.

Her parents were yelling at each other in the kitchen, and the occasional bump into the wall caused the pictures to bounce back and forth. She muted the TV to hear what they were saying.

"I'm so sick of this!" her mother screamed, slamming the fridge door.

The familiar sound of a bottle of beer opening echoed into the living room.

"Sure! Have another drink!" her father yelled back, slapping the kitchen table and laughing.

There was a moment of silence and then the screaming started again.

"You're such a disappointing father…if we could even call you a father!" her mother said, going silent, and Reena could hear her taking a sip of her beer. "How many other bitches have you fucked?!" she yelled in her slurred voice.

"You should talk," her father replied. "You're nothing but a bad example! Wrecking our family and blaming me. You're the disappointment!"

There was a smashing sound from the kitchen and the wall seemed to jump in place. The pictures fell and smashed on the floor.

Reena pulled the blanket up to her chin and pushed herself further down into the couch. She turned the sound on the TV back on and turned to look towards the kitchen doorway.

There was another loud thud on the wall and another crashing sound, followed by some muffled screaming. A moment later, Reena heard her father scream and then saw him fall to the floor, his hand visible from where she was on the couch.

"You bitch!" her father yelled as he pulled himself up. "I'm bleeding!"

He jumped to his feet and disappeared into the kitchen.

There was a loud slap and a gasp from her mother. Another loud bang followed, the sound of someone falling to the floor, and then silence.

"Come at me again and I'll kill you," her mother screamed as she opened the silverware drawer and removed something.

Reena jumped up from the couch and ran towards the kitchen. Her heart was pounding and she felt weak with fright, but she stepped further until she could see what had happened.

The first thing she noticed was all the blood. The laminate floor was coated in bright red, and it was streaked across the kitchen counters, with small pools formed everywhere. The walls were covered with it, and the occasional handprint was visible. The kitchen table had been overturned and there was glass everywhere. Pieces of broken beer bottles were scattered around, and the ashtray had been flung across the kitchen and broke one of the cupboard doors.

In the corner of the room lay her father, conscious, but badly hurt. His head was bleeding profusely and he was cradling his hand. Several fingers were bent at odd angles.

Reena eyed her mother and became frightened by what she saw. In her hand was a large knife, the light shining off its sharp edge. Her mother was panting like an animal, sweat covering her forehead. She was enraged at that moment, and her eyes pierced through Reena.

"Go to your room!" she screamed at her, pointing the tip of the knife towards her.

She took a step back and stopped.

"Go! Now!" her father screamed as he glanced towards her mother.

Reena took another step back and hesitated, staring into the kitchen. Turning, she ran up the stairs to her room, shutting her door quietly and sitting on her bed.

Around her room, there were several pictures of the family as they use to be. Times when they were happy and everything seemed right. A trip to the zoo, all of them posing in front of the elephant enclosure, another one of them swimming together at a beach, and one at a birthday party where all of them were wearing party hats and eating cake.

They used to be so close and full of love. They would go to the movies every weekend in the afternoon as a family, visiting their local small-town theater, The Oasis, and laugh together. Afterwards, they would spend the day shopping, touring the town, getting ice cream, and have dinner as a family. It was always a perfect day.

That changed when Reena was nine. Her father had an affair, and when her mother found out, she became a different person. The day it happened, Reena had been sick at school and her mother picked her up. They came home, and both of them could hear what was happening in the bedroom. Her parents went to counselling together to try and mend the crack that was formed, but it didn't work.

Soon after, her mother started drinking heavily. Their family time was replaced by cases of beer, and both Reena and her father suffered. Within a few months, her father developed an addiction to drugs, and it destroyed the family. Her mother stopped going to work and spent her days sleeping and drinking, and her father began working less; spending more time alone in the basement of the house and disconnecting from Reena and her mother completely.

One day, Reena crept into the basement and watched him. He held a pipe to his mouth and used a lighter to heat the bulbous end. He breathed in deeply and held his breath. As he exhaled, he caught Reena's eyes with his and she froze. A moment passed and he turned from her, flicking the lighter again as she crawled up the stairs and left him alone.

Reena jumped as a loud knock sounded on her door and it slowly opened. A police officer came into view and he looked through the room while he came towards Reena.

"Hi, Reena. My name's Brad," he said, sitting next to her on the bed.

Reena smiled and looked at him, noticing the gun in his holster and the handcuffs that were tucked into his belt.

"Hi," she said, timidly.

"Are you okay?" he asked.

She nodded and paused. "We've met before," she said, looking up at his face.

"Have we?" he asked, raising an eyebrow.

"Yes, you've been here before."

He smiled. "Yes, I remember. A few months ago, right?"

Reena nodded. During that visit, the police determined it wasn't serious. The difference between that fight and this one was that there was no ignoring the blood and broken furniture.

"And now you're back...you must think we're an awful family," she said.

Brad shook his head and rested his hand on her shoulder. "Sometimes people need help, and we're here to do just that."

Reena heard a noise in the hallway and stood up. Brad grabbed for her arm, but she twisted off his grip and walked into the hallway.

Her mother and father were being escorted out of the house, and Reena noticed that her mother was handcuffed.

She sighed and turned towards Brad. "I don't think you can help us."

A week later, her mother was given a twelve-month probation sentence and Reena was put into a foster home.

She was placed into a new home with overly loving parents; Jack and Maria, as well as two other foster children: Ronda, who was eighteen, and Ethan, who was seventeen. They got along well, and after a while, it didn't feel like there was anything but a natural bond between the three of them. She hadn't realized how much she'd enjoy having a brother and sister, and she wouldn't trade it for anything.

Every two weeks, she was accompanied by a Child Protective Services agent to visit her parents, who were still living together, in a public place. The visits always went the same. Her mother would confess that she had issues and would plead that she would change her ways, and her father would shyly admit he had his problems, and acknowledge that he needed to change his ways, too.

Five months into her new home, she received a call from her mother. Reena's father had passed away. A drug overdose after a particularly hard drug binge. She had found him in the basement of their house, hunched over a desk. That day, she had awoken and noticed a slight odour and followed it, discovering that he had been dead for a few days. Reena knew, without asking, that her mother hadn't noticed because she had been on her own drinking binge and barely knew what day it was.

Reena breathed for a minute, waiting to feel sadness creep into her. It didn't, and she wondered if something was wrong with her, if maybe she had already mourned her father two years earlier, as he slipped into drug abuse and changed into a different person.

"Reena?" her mother asked, her voice slurring. "Are you there?"

Reena paused. "Yes, I am," she said, her teeth grinding together. "I want you to leave me alone. Don't call again, and don't look for me."

Her mother screamed and began pleading. "I can change! I can change!"

Reena shook her head. "Goodbye, Cheryl." She pulled the phone from her ear and hit the end call button, letting a deep exhale release from her lungs. It was the last time she spoke to her.

On her eighteenth birthday, Jack and Maria presented her with a new car and tuition for her nursing degree. Ronda and Ethan came back home for her birthday, and she couldn't have been happier. Ronda moved out a few years earlier to start her engineering degree, and Ethan moved to Chicago with his girlfriend. They kept in touch, but it was never the same.

After her graduation, she applied for as many jobs as she could, and within a month, she got a job as a nurse at Mount Sinai downtown. She had been hired on full-time, with the strict warning to try, at all costs, to avoid burnout and to always be attentive.

She had grown to love her job at the hospital, and now that her drive to solidify her career ambitions was met, she could look towards the rest of her future.

Her coworkers helped her set up blind dates every so often, but no one ever struck her as the person she was meant to be with. She was a believer in fate and knew that when she found the man she was supposed to be with, she would know. Undoubtedly, full heartedly, she would know. After two years of disastrous blind dates and countless dead ends, something happened.

The hospital was having renovations done. Walls were being torn down, ceilings were being fixed. The furniture was being removed and replaced, and the electrical system was being redone.

One day, she walked into the nurse's station and saw a man on a ladder who had wires in his hand and was cursing at whatever he was doing. She nodded to him, and then paid no attention. The patient she was dealing with was being difficult and making her day a bad one.

"Excuse me," the man said, speaking towards the top of her head.

She looked up and noticed that he was pointing towards the ground below the ladder.

"Can you pass me that?" he asked, wiggling his finger towards a piece of paper.

She bent down and picked it up, and as she passed it to him their hands brushed against one another.

She looked over his body, admiring his thin muscular frame, and when he looked up to the ceiling she couldn't help herself from smiling.

He turned back and looked down at her. "I'm Alan," he said, extending his hand.

"Reena," she replied, shaking it. "It's nice to meet you."

Fate, it seemed, was doing its job.

4

"Welcome to The Laelynn," a man said pleasantly as he opened the metal gates, a thick Spanish accent accentuating his words. His white shirt was opened at the collar and neatly tucked into his gray pants. On the left side of his chest was a pin; two concentric black circles.

He extended his hand and pointed up a set of brick stairs. "Please, follow me," he said, standing up onto the first set of steps. "You can leave your bags here and our staff will be pleased to take them to your rooms."

The Laelynn was an impressive building. Five stories high and its tallest peaks seemed to cut the sky open with their sharp points. The brickwork around the windows was intricate, but curiously, all the windows were barred.

The grounds surrounding the hotel were well manicured and full of bright flowers. Tall trees surrounded it, and tiny shrubs lined each of the walkways leading from the main entrance. The perimeter wall was covered with thick vines.

"What's with the bars?" Alan asked, pointing towards them.

Reena shrugged. "Maybe security?"

He nodded as he looked around the property.

"It's a nice feeling knowing we'll be safe this week," Reena reasoned.

He nodded again, seemingly taken aback by the imposing nature of the hotel. "It feels more like a gated community than a resort," he said, looking towards her.

"It does, but -" She was interrupted mid-sentence by the

concierge from the main gate.

"Please, come this way," he said, beckoning them.

They followed, briefly stopping to notice a symbol on the façade of the hotel, just above the entrance. Two concentric black circles. The same as the concierge's pin.

"Excuse me," Reena said, pointing to the symbol. "What is that design?"

He looked at it and smiled. "Oh, it's just a design that the owners came up with long ago," he said.

Alan looked at Reena and raised his eyebrows.

The inside of the hotel was filled with modern paintings and furnishings. The white and grey tiled floor sparkled as the sunlight from the windows fell on it, nearly blinding them.

Imposing archways lined the hallway that led to the first level rooms, and as Alan looked down them, they seemed to stretch forever.

"It seems so humble," he said, turning towards Reena.

She laughed and continued following the concierge.

As they approached the desk, she thanked him for his help.

"No problem," he said, "I was happy to help."

As he turned to walk away, she stopped him. "What's your name?" she asked.

"My name is Luis," he said as he hurried away, following another set of guests down one of the hallways.

"Next please," the woman behind the desk said, ushering for them to come forward.

"Hola!" Alan said as he stepped towards the desk.

The woman laughed. "Buenos tardes!" she said. "A little Spanish goes a long way in Mexico, but every staff member at the hotel is fluent in English as well."

Alan laughed and made a gesture to wipe his forehead. "That's good, because I've already exhausted my Spanish."

"What name is the reservation under?" she asked.

"Mr. and Mrs. Trino," he said.

The woman typed for a moment and then turned around and grabbed a stack of papers. She handed them to him. "Here are your room keys, our welcome package, information related to all of our activities, and your wi-fi password." She continued. "Also, we would like to let you know that hotel policy states that if you leave the grounds and venture into private land, we are no longer responsible for your well-being. Do either of you have any questions?"

They shook their heads. "Not at the moment," Reena said, turning to look down the hallway.

"Well then, let me find Luis and he can show you to your room," the woman said before she disappeared down the same hallway Luis went down.

"What do you think?" Alan asked Reena.

"It's nice," she said, a question mark almost audible in her response.

He shuffled his feet. "You don't like it?"

"I do," she said. "I'm just a bit tired from the flight and the bus ride. John and Lily didn't exactly take the hint that eyes being closed means someone typically wants some sleep."

He laughed. "I'm a bit tired too," he said, glancing at his watch. It was three-thirty. "Why don't we unpack and see about a nap, then we can have dinner and take a walk to the beach."

She nodded. "That's a good plan."

After a few more minutes, Luis came hurriedly around the corner.

"My apologies," he said, looking behind him at the receptionist, who was staring at him disapprovingly. "I'm new here and I made a mistake. I shouldn't have left you so soon."

Reena touched his forearm. "There's no need to apologize," she said, noticing that the receptionist was still watching him. "Really, there's no need to be sorry."

"Come with me and I'll show you where your room is," he said, guiding them towards an elevator across from the main desk.

"So, Luis," Alan said, as they stood inside the elevator. "How long have you been here?"

He cleared his throat. "I've been here for three months," he said, rubbing his hands against his pants.

"Is your wife here, too?" Reena asked, motioning towards the wedding ring on his left hand.

"Oh," he said, twisting the wedding band. "No, unfortunately. She passed away just over three months ago. It's just my daughter, Ava, and I. She just turned five."

Reena sighed. "I'm sorry," she said.

"It's okay," he said. "She worked in the hotel actually."

Alan looked at him curiously.

"There was an accident and she died. It was just off the grounds."

Reena looked at him sympathetically.

"After her funeral, I was offered her job by Hugh," he said, as the elevator opened at the top floor.

Reena stepped up to Luis' side as they walked. "So, after your wife passed away, Hugh hired you to fill her position?"

He laughed. "It does sound a bit strange, but yes, that's what happened. Hugh offered it to me and now my daughter and I live and work here."

Reena stopped as he turned towards them.

"You live here?" she asked.

"We all do. All of the hotel staff live on the basement level."

She looked at Alan and frowned. "The basement?"

"Yes," Luis said. "It's actually very nice down there. We all have our own rooms, there's no rent, and we're never late for work." He laughed to himself.

As he inserted the master key card into their door, Alan heard a faint growl behind him. He turned and saw a German Shepherd, walking backwards from him. He moved a bit closer and the dog turned, showing a large cut several inches long in its neck that appeared fresh. He took another step and the dog turned and ran down the hallway, disappearing behind the corner of the wall.

"Please," Luis interrupted, touching Alan's elbow. "This is your room."

He nodded and stepped through the doorway.

Inside, they were greeted by a bright and spacious room. The bed was king size, dressed in crisp white sheets with a bouquet of bright red and pink flowers on top of it. At the side of the room was a desk with a phone, and on either side of the bed was a nightstand. A large dresser sat against the wall across from the bed.

"Is there anything I can get you?" Luis asked.

"No, I think we're good," Reena said as she looked through the room.

He nodded and turned to leave. "Oh," he said, "just a reminder, breakfast is offered downstairs in the dining room from seven until nine, lunch is offered from eleven until one, and dinner is offered from five until seven.”

“That sounds great,” Alan said, lifting his suitcases onto the bed.

Luis smiled and turned, walking through the doorway and shutting the door gently.

They spent the next half hour unpacking their suitcases; filling the dresser drawers with their clothing, and then arranging everything the way they wanted it.

“It’s nap time,” Reena announced as she closed the closet door.

Alan nodded and climbed into bed, shuffling beneath the blankets. He held them up and looked at her. “Are you coming?” he asked, shimmying his shoulders.

She smiled and set an alarm for an hour before swinging her feet under the covers and resting her head on the pillow. Within minutes, both of them were sleeping.

Reena blinked and rolled over, noticing Alan staring at her.

“Hello, Sleeping Beauty,” he said, yawning loudly.

“What time is it?” she asked, sitting up in bed.

“It’s six. I let you sleep a little longer,” he said, moving his feet to the floor as he yawned again. “Did you have good dreams?”

She paused for a moment. “I don’t think I even dreamt,” she said, slowly getting out of bed. “Did you have a good sleep?”

He shook his head. “Not a great one.”

She frowned. “That’s too bad. We’ll try and get to bed earlier tonight then,” she said, standing and looking out the windows which gave a view of the front grounds. The security bars were a nuisance for the view.

“Are you hungry?” he asked, walking to her side.

“I’m starving.” She rubbed her stomach. “Let’s go down and get something to eat.”

They each put some comfortable clothing on and left the room.

Alan recalled the dog he had seen and paused, wondering what happened to it.

“Are you coming?” Reena called to him as the elevator door opened.

He nodded and followed, slipping past her as she glanced to where he had been looking.

"What did you see?" she asked, letting the elevator doors shut.

"Nothing," he said, brushing off an uneasy feeling.

On the fifth floor, the doors opened and Luis stepped inside. He greeted them with a bright smile.

"Hola!" he said. "Did you get all of your belongings unpacked?"

Reena nodded. "Yes, we did."

He smiled. "That's good. Now it's dinner time?"

"We're both starving," Alan said.

"The dinner here is a very good one," Luis said, turning towards the door as the elevator slowed. "It's buffet style, more food than you can imagine."

The door slid open and he exited, turning around quickly. "The dining room is down this hallway," he pointed. "Take a left and then a right at the end of that hallway. Enjoy your dinner!"

They followed his directions and found the dining room. It was empty, except for two other tables with two people at each, and they chose a seat next to one of the barred windows that looked out onto the surrounding wall of the hotel.

Reena set her phone down and turned towards the food, which sat on large tables covered by heat lamps.

"Are you coming?" she asked Alan, who was seemingly staring off into space.

He nodded and followed her. They both admired the selection of food and quickly served themselves, rushing back to their table to eat. It was divided into cuisines; Chinese, Mexican, Italian, and American. At the end was a section dedicated to desserts.

They decided to take a walk to the beach. The sun was setting to their left, and it illuminated the road to the beach in dark orange and yellow light.

"This is beautiful," Reena said, grabbing Alan's hand and swinging both of them together.

"Not as beautiful as you," he said meaningfully, pulling her hand up and kissing the top of it.

"What should we do tomorrow?" she asked him.

"We should go to Sun Garden Resort and see what the shopping is all about," he said, noticing someone walking out of a driveway up ahead.

"That's a good idea," she said. She also noticed the man up ahead.

As they got closer, they saw that he was wearing one of the uniforms from the hotel, complete with the pin on his chest.

He greeted them. "Hola! How are you two this evening?"

They nodded in unison. "Very well, thank you."

The man bowed his head slightly and stood in place, watching them as they kept going.

"I wonder what he's doing out here?" Reena said as she took her eyes from the driveway and looked out onto the ocean. The movement of the waves was hypnotizing, and the smell of it was relaxing.

Alan turned and looked behind him. There was a truck parked further back, which hadn't been there before. He saw the shape of a figure in the driver's seat.

"That's odd," he said. Reena followed his gaze. "That wasn't there when we walked past, and if he drove up, he was quiet about it."

"That's a little strange," she said, not seeming to care.

As they approached the beach, another hotel employee walked by. She nodded at them and kept walking up the road towards the hotel.

"Let's go closer to the water," Alan said, stepping towards it. He reached down and removed his sandals. He stepped into the moist, cool sand and pushed his feet far in.

Reena did the same, enjoying the feeling of the sand between her toes. The chill of it felt relaxing.

He noticed a bench further up the beach and pulled her hand as he started walking to it. They sat down and looked out over the ocean. The waves crashed lightly as the sky became darker towards the east.

He put his arm around her and she leaned into him, breathing in the scent of his faded cologne and the fresh mist of ocean that floated their way.

"This is going to be a great week," she said, closing her eyes.

$$5$$

Alan and Reena sat in the dining room, observing the other guests at the hotel. They had been there over an hour, enjoying coffee after their breakfast, and had only seen five other people.

"I wonder where everyone is?" he asked, blowing on his coffee. It was strong and bitter, but he drank it anyways.

"There weren't many people who got off the bus with us," she replied, eyeing the others in the room.

He nodded and took a sip. "Still though, was there no one else staying at the hotel before we arrived?"

"Our week here starts today, Sunday, and ends on Saturday. Maybe there's a cycle here. A week and then you're gone," Reena said.

Alan nodded.

Some employees entered the room and walked to the buffet, removing the half-empty trays and carrying them to the kitchen.

Alan set his cup down. "Should we go? I want to get some shopping done."

She nodded and stood up, taking a final sip of her coffee before setting the cup down on the table.

There was a bang of metal pans echoing from the buffet table. They both turned to see Luis fumbling with the remainder of trays that hadn't yet slipped from his hands and hit the floor.

As Alan and Reena approached him to help, a tall man walked from the kitchen and up to him. He was wearing a tailored black suit, a dark purple tie, and polished black shoes. He stood over Luis and stared.

"What happened?" asked the man.

Luis looked up and froze. His face lost all color and turned sickly pale.

The man shifted again and crossed his arms, his bony elbows poking through his suit.

"Luis!" he yelled, his voice carrying through the dining room.

Luis fumbled again and lost another tray. "I'm sorry," he said to the man. "I dropped these by accident."

The man shuffled once again and turned to look at Alan and Reena, who stood still with blank expressions on their faces. He didn't acknowledge their presence and looked down at Luis again. "Clean it up, quickly, and then come and see me," he said, before turning away and disappearing back into the kitchen.

Luis was visibly upset and nervous. They could see that he was shaking. They walked over to him and bent down to help.

"No," he said, lightly brushing their hands from the mess on the floor. "This is my accident and I will clean it."

Reena reached down and started cleaning as he gently touched her hand and looked at her. "If he comes back and you're helping, it'll be worse."

She pulled her hand back. "Who is he?" she asked.

Luis looked at the entrance to the kitchen. "That's Hugh," he said, returning to the mess on the floor.

Alan adjusted his kneeling position. "Hugh seems like an asshole," he said.

Luis gave a brief smile and looked around. "He is, but he's my boss and I have no choice but to listen."

Reena was about to say something when Hugh appeared again. "Quickly," he said and left the room.

"Please, let me clean this," Luis said as he used his hand to wave them away.

They stood up and took a step back, hesitating.

"I'll be fine," Luis said, smiling.

They spent the morning walking the streets of Sun Garden Resort, going into the many giftshops. Most of the gifts were the same, with the only difference being the name of the shop on them. Pens, buttons, bracelets, and blank journals lined the shelves.

"Why are so many giftshops so tacky?" Alan asked, looking over the merchandise. There were old movies, some film reel decorations, and some cookbooks all jammed together on one display.

"Because they can be. There's always a sucker out there willing to buy something ugly," Reena commented, flipping through a stack of shirts bedazzled with the name of the resort.

"Well I'm hungry. Let's not be one of those suckers," he said, walking to the doorway of the giftshop and waiting for her.

"There's a little restaurant over there," she said, starting to walk towards it as he followed.

They approached the restaurant and opened the door, smelling the sweet aroma of fresh baking Inside, they sat on a bench and waited to be seated.

"Did you notice that this resort is filled with people?" he asked, admiring the decorations inside.

"Yeah, I noticed that," she said. "You were right when you said that ours is empty."

The restaurant was busy. All the tables were either full or dirty from being used. Several servers poked their heads out into the waiting area and apologized for the delay.

"I'm so sorry!" a young woman said as she walked up to them. "Just the two of you?"

She guided them through the restaurant, seating them next to a window that overlooked the main street.

"My name is Victoria, and I'll be your server today," she said brightly, showing off a big smile. She removed a pad of paper from her apron and clicked a pen, asking, "What can I get you to drink?"

They ordered their drinks and then their meal, enjoying the relaxing afternoon they were having. Afterwards, they toured the resort a bit more before heading back to their hotel, struggling to carry their purchases up the roadway.

"It looks like you've had a busy day of shopping," Luis said as they entered the hotel.

They laughed and set their bags on the ground.

"Are you alright?" Reena asked him. "I hope you weren't in too much trouble from Hugh."

He nodded. "I'm good, but thanks for your concern."

Alan reached forward and patted Luis' back. He flinched and

grimaced as if in pain.

"What's wrong?" Alan asked, wondering if he had hit his back harder than he intended.

"Oh, it's nothing. I was careless and tripped on the stairs. I seem to have pulled something in my back."

Reena frowned. She wasn't sure whether she believed him.

"Are you sure that's what's wrong?" she asked. "I'm a nurse, let me take a look."

He shook his head. "I'm fine," he said. "I'll be watching how I walk on the stairs from now on," he joked before he turned and briskly walked away.

She watched him disappear out of sight. "Do you believe him?" she asked Alan.

He shook his head. "No, but what can we do?"

She agreed and reached down to grab the bags beside her. "Let's go put this away and then take a swim in the ocean," she said.

He picked up his bags and excitedly followed her.

After their swim, they spent the rest of the day at the beach, lounging around. The hours seemed to pass quickly, and soon they found that it was almost dinner time.

They returned to the hotel and had a nice meal. They opted for the Chinese buffet and planned the hike that they intended to take the next day.

"There's a trail that leads through the forest behind the hotel," Alan said, recalling what he had read in the hotel's information package.

Reena nodded as she sipped her wine. "That sounds great," she said.

As they spoke, the receptionist approached them. "May I clear your table for you?" she asked, leaning over and picking up the plates and empty glasses.

Reena thanked her. "What's your name?" she asked the woman.

"Elena," she said, turning and abruptly leaving.

As they watched her walk to the kitchen, Hugh approached her. He grabbed some of the dishes from her hands.

"That's odd," Reena said. "He was so rude to Luis."

Once they were done with dinner, they decided to have an early night and went up to their room.

"I need a shower," Alan said, stripping his clothes off. "Do you want to come?" he asked her.

Reena threw her clothes off and walked ahead of him into the bathroom.

"I guess that's a yes," he said, shutting the door as she turned on the water.

Inside the shower, they began kissing. He rubbed her body, feeling the contours of her with his palms.

"You're beautiful," he said, pressing his hips into her.

She smiled and tilted her head backwards, allowing the water to rinse off the salty ocean that lingered in her hair. Alan passed her the soap after he had cleaned himself, helping her by rubbing her back.

"Let's get out of here," he said, rinsing as quickly as he could.

She did the same, and soon they found themselves in their bed, kissing each other and laughing.

He reached to his night stand and opened it, pulling out the box of condoms. He removed one and put the rest away. The foil package crinkled as he opened it and slipped it on, failing to notice the small holes that had been poked into the package and the condom itself.

She clicked the light off, and he slowly lowered himself onto her and then into her.

A groan followed each thrust, and they were both fully enveloped in euphoria, intensely focused on one another.

In the corner of the room, in the shallow light the moon provided, the wall began to buckle and move. A black figure slowly emerged from it, pulling the wallpaper with it as it solidified into a human shape. Its body was partially decomposed, bringing with it a chill that swept through the room.

Pure white eyes, piercing and without pupils, focused on them. It stood, staring intently and wavering slightly. It didn't blink, and the only sounds were the breathing of Alan and Reena. Once they finished, it bent backwards and crawled back into the wall, disappearing from sight while the wallpaper smoothed itself and the creases disappeared.

6

Alan laughed as his father dove for the roast as it fell from the oven. As his mother pulled it out, she dropped it and sent the roast flying through the air. She was preparing dinner for the family to celebrate Alan's sixteenth birthday.

"I got it!" his father yelled, jumping towards it but landing on the counter and sending dishes crashing to the ground. The sound of his mother's infectious laugh sounded off the walls.

"Well, I tried," his father said as he bent down to pick up the broken dishes.

Alan got the broom and swept the small bits of glass and the food that had spilled, and his mother wiped the grease on the floor.

"What's for dinner now?" he asked, emptying the dustpan in the trash.

"It's your birthday," his mother said. "Why don't you decide."

He thought for a moment. He looked at his father, who was standing behind his mother, and saw him silently mouth the word, pizza.

He laughed. "Why don't we just order pizza" he said.

His mother sighed. "If that's what you want, but I really wanted to make a nice dinner for your sixteenth."

He smiled. "It's okay, Mom!"

"I'll call and order supper," his father said, reaching for the phone and dialing. As it rang, he walked into the living room.

"Are you sure that's what you want?" his mother asked.

Alan nodded. "Yes, Mom, pizza is just fine."

His father came back into the kitchen and announced that dinner would be there in thirty minutes.

"That's perfect," his mother said as she walked to his father and stood beside him. "Alan, we want to give you your gift now," she said, extending her arm for him.

She pushed him forward and outside; along the walkway from the backdoor to the garage.

As they opened the door, his father said, "It's not brand new, but it'll work for now."

He clicked on the light, and a truck became visible. It was a black Ford, only a few years old.

Alan ran to it and jokingly hugged it. "Are you serious?" he asked, pleading to know if it was a joke.

"It's certainly not for us," his mother laughed. "Now you won't have to use ours."

"Thank you, thank you, thank you," he said, opening the driver's side door. On the seat were the keys, an envelope, and inside was a card with five hundred dollars in it.

"Sixteen is a big birthday," his dad said, "and we're proud of you for working, doing well in school, and helping us around here."

They had decided to do renovations on the house throughout the summer and Alan and his father had done the laborious work, leaving the painting and decorating to his mother. A month into the renovations, his father had lost some clients at work and their budget was thinned down. Alan bought more of the supplies needed to finish the work, and now that his father had his clientele built back up, they wanted to repay him.

"Well, thank you," he said, hugging both of his parents.

As the summer progressed, Alan didn't slow down with touring the city in his truck. After work, he would take random drives, relaxing for a while before heading home. It had become normal for his dinner to be waiting in the oven, and his parents to be asleep on the couch.

One day, he came home to his father preparing dinner while his mother rested.

"This is a change," he said, walking to his father to offer any help he could.

"Yeah, your mother wasn't feeling well and needed a nap," his dad said, frowning.

"Is she okay?"

"Oh yea," his father said, jokingly messing up his hair. "She's fine."

A few weeks later, Alan's father called him in the middle of his shift at work. He was panicked.

"I'm going to take your mother to the hospital," he said, his voice loud and filled with worry.

"What happened?!" Alan asked, disappearing into a private room.

"She collapsed. Her stomach was hurting badly and then she fell," his father said. "I'll see you later."

Alan returned to work but couldn't focus. He left within an hour and went to the hospital. After getting directions from the receptionist, he navigated the complicated hallways, asking a few nurses for clarification. He walked under a sign that read oncology, and entered a room. It was a small waiting room, and his father was sitting in a corner by himself.

"Did they say what's wrong?" he asked, sitting next to him.

"No, not yet," his father said, his face filled with worry.

"I'm sure it'll be fine," Alan said, trying to sound convincing.

A doctor called them into a private room.

"I'm Dr. Elliott," she said as she sat down. "I was reviewing your wife's file and talking with her. We've run some tests and we've reached a likely diagnosis." She paused for a moment, staring at them. "It's stomach cancer."

Alan immediately turned to his father. His face was pale and blank.

"We've passed her file onto the oncologist and he's going to review it and update us with his findings in a few days," she said softly. "If you need someone to talk to, we can arrange a counselling service."

"No, I'll be fine," his father said abruptly. He turned to Alan after a moment and asked, "Would you like to talk with someone?"

Alan shook his head. "I'm fine."

They met with the oncologist a few days later.

"My name is Dr. Andrews," he said. "We've reviewed your wife's file that was sent by Dr. Elliott." He shuffled some papers and coughed to clear his throat. "We've determined that it is stomach cancer, and unfortunately, very advanced. It's stage four."

His father thought for a moment. "It's terminal?"

"Yes," Dr. Andrews said, lowering his head slightly. "We can recommend chemotherapy to slow the progression, but that can be a difficult scenario. It comes down to quality and quantity. An aggressive treatment plan can slow it down and possibly add a few months, but the quality of time that she has may suffer. The alternative is to skip treatment and focus on symptom control."

His father breathed deeply. "Add a few months?" he asked, looking at the floor.

The doctor nodded. "Yes. If I was going to give a prognosis, I would say that your wife has about two months to live."

It was like a sledgehammer had hit Alan in the chest.

"I want to talk this over with my wife," his father said.

Dr. Andrews nodded. "Of course," he said. "Whenever you're ready, we can do that."

Later that day, Alan and his father sat with his mother and discussed what was happening. It was decided that she would forgo any treatment and instead have them control the pain and help her to be as comfortable as possible.

She died a month and a half later, Alan and his father by her side. It was early afternoon and the flowers in her room were at full bloom. The air was sweet with their smell, and she lay sleeping. She was calm and comfortable, tucked in tightly with blankets surrounding her; the odd teddy bear amongst the blankets, offering its own type of comfort.

"We'll see her again," his father said, rubbing her hand gently. "I don't know where or how, but we will."

Alan nodded. "I know," he said.

A moment later, the heart rate monitor made a beep and then paused. A few minutes more, and it beeped continuously. A nurse came in, checked for a pulse and then left quickly. She returned with Dr. Elliott, and after some more checks of his mother, they looked at Alan and his father.

They stood and made their way out. Alan left first and waited in the hallway for his father. A few minutes passed, and then his father slowly shut the door. He held his hand on the cool metal for a long moment, before letting it slide off.

"Goodbye, Mom," Alan said softly to himself as he followed his father down the long hallway.

Alan had wondered, before this moment, how he would feel. He wondered if he'd be distraught or calm. He knew he'd be sad, but he wasn't sure what the secondary emotions would be. It turned out, he felt relief. Relief that his mother had peacefully moved on, and relief that the emotional torture his father was feeling would now be able to start healing.

A few months later, the financial tolls started to appear. The bills were far behind, and Alan's father began working many hours of overtime. It was becoming normal for neither of them to see each other. He owned an electrical company and took any jobs he could to bring home more money.

"Dad, this is for you," he said one day as his father came home. He handed him a check.

"Where did this come from?" his father asked, holding the check in one hand and his other hand in the air.

"You're killing yourself by working so much. I sold my truck."

His father paused for a moment and then handed the check back to him.

"No," his father said. "You take this money and either see if you can get the truck back or go buy something else."

Alan shook his head. "I wanted to help. It's my choice, not yours," he said firmly, handing it back to his father, who didn't make a gesture to take it from him.

He set it on the counter. "It's staying there. I don't want it. I want to help out and I should be able to."

His father hesitated as he reached for it. "This would pay off everything."

Alan nodded. "I know," he said. "I looked at all the bills and you'd actually be left with a couple thousand."

His father thought for a moment and then hugged him, holding him for a few minutes.

After awhile, with encouragement from Alan, his father began dating again. "There's someone for everyone, and you deserve to find her," he told him, meaning every word.

It was around his eighteenth birthday when his father met a woman, and they dated for a few months before Alan was introduced to her. She was friendly, warm, and above all, she made his father feel complete. Her name was Julie, and Alan liked her.

Once he graduated, he accepted his father's offer to become an electrician and focused the next few years on it. Financially stable, happy, and newly married, his father eventually sold his company to Alan and took an early retirement.

Three years after buying the company, Alan took a job at Mount Sinai downtown to rewire one of the floors the hospital was having renovated.

On the first day, he stood on a ladder, fumbling with a set of wires. He had notes written on a piece of paper and dropped it. "Fuck," he said as a nurse walked in and stared up at him. She nodded quickly and then turned away.

He looked down at her after a moment and then asked her to hand him the paper.

She bent down and grabbed it, their hands brushing as she passed it to him.

He turned to her and introduced himself. "I'm Alan."

"I'm Reena," she said.

7

After lunch, Alan and Reena got ready for their hike. He filled two bottles of water and handed one to her.

"Are you ready?" he asked her.

She adjusted her shoes and tied them tighter. "Ready as I'll ever be," she said, sprinting over to her suitcase and grabbing her camera.

"Let's take the stairs," he said as they left their room.

They entered the stairwell and let the solid metal door slam shut behind them. Reena stopped and looked at the handle. On the outside of the door was a thick metal lock with a small keyhole in it.

"Look at this," she said, beckoning him back up the stairs. "Isn't that odd?"

"Most hotels have locks like this," he said, not seeming to care about it.

"This thick though?" she asked, brushing the lock with her hand.

"It's just a lock," he said, walking down a few steps. "Let's go."

She followed, turning back to look at it. As they passed the other floors, the same lock was on the outside of all the doors.

"Ignore it," he said impatiently.

"Are you alright?" she asked him as he kept descending the stairs faster than she could keep up.

"I'm fine," he said, finally stopping to allow her to catch up.

"Are you sure?" she asked, watching him for any signs of anger.

"I'm fine," he said again. "I just want to go for a hike."

She nodded and followed, feeling a slight uneasiness as they exited the stairwell and made their way across the lobby.

Elena watched from behind the desk, inspecting them as they left and ventured outside.

They walked their way along the pathway that took them into the forested area.

He reached for her and grabbed her hand. She hesitated and then grasped his.

"You're good now?" she asked.

He slowed his pace and looked at her. "Of course I am. Why do you ask?"

"You seemed really irritable," she said. "You didn't seem like yourself."

"I didn't mean to be." He said. He leaned over and kissed her on the cheek.

She thought for a moment and then smiled, brushing off his mannerisms from earlier. She knew he would tell her if anything was wrong.

They kept walking, enjoying the wilderness that spread out around them. Birds flew overhead, chirping as they flew from branch to branch, occasionally swooping to the ground to grab a bug from the dirt.

"It's nice out here," he said.

"We're so used to the city that we forget what it's like to actually be outside," she said, removing the lens cover from the camera and turning it on. She pointed to a large tree covered in moss. "Go stand over there."

He walked over and she took a few pictures. He used his hands to make shapes around his head. "Quit voguing," she said, making him laugh.

As they walked, the pathway abruptly turned and continued towards their right.

"Let's go this way," he said, looking through a small opening in the bushes that led straight but was largely overgrown with branches.

"Through there?" she asked.

He stepped into the opening and bent some branches out of the way. "Why not? Let's make our own path."

She followed, swatting some leaves that swung down and stayed close to him.

After almost a half an hour of walking, the trees stopped and opened onto a cleared area. It was square, with all of the trees perfectly cut down and a large dirt pile to one side. In the center was an open pit.

"What's this?" Reena wondered as she stepped up onto the dirt pile, looking down into the open area.

Alan followed. "Construction maybe," he said, looking around and noticing a roadway that came into the cleared area.

The tire tracks were fresh, and he noticed that the dirt in the pit was too. There was a black powdery substance covering the ground, and when he looked more closely at it, he realized it was soot.

"Everything is covered in soot," he said, pointing at the ground. "Maybe they're building something else out here," he said as he stepped down off of the pile and walked to something sitting on the edge of the pit.

He picked it up with the tips of his fingers, holding it to examine it.

"What's that?" Reena asked as she walked towards him.

He handed it to her and she held it up. "Someone's torn shirt?" she asked, dropping it quickly.

"Look at all of this," she said, showing her hands to him. They were covered in soot.

"Burning pits aren't that uncommon," he said, taking a sip of water. "Maybe they burn their garbage."

She swatted at her legs to scatter the bugs and looked at her watch. They had been walking for close to two hours and she was tired.

"Come down, please!" they heard when they approached the main gates of the hotel. There was a loud commotion occurring outside.

As they entered, they noticed a small group of hotel employees and a couple guests standing outside on the grass, looking up.

Alan and Reena followed their gaze and recognized John, visibly upset, standing on the edge of the roof.

Reena gasped and stopped walking. "What's he doing?!" she asked as she felt a burst of fear move through her.

Alan stumbled over his words. "I have no idea."

"Where's my wife?!" John screamed from the roof. "Where is

she?!”

The hotel employees seemed nervous.

“I haven’t seen her since last night!” he yelled, pacing back and forth on the edge.

“Please, come down and we can talk!” Elena called from the ground.

He shook his head. “No! You tell me where she is!”

Elena turned to another employee and they talked briefly, then the employee ran into the hotel.

“There’s something weird going on here!” he yelled again, standing still. “This place is dangerous!” He turned around and looked further up the roof.

“Sir, please come down!” Elena yelled.

He hesitated and looked behind him. “What happens if I do?” he said.

Elena looked as the employee came back out and ran up to her. They exchanged some words.

“We found her!” Elena yelled to John.

He shook his head. “I don’t believe you!” he yelled, rubbing his face to get rid of the sweat that was starting to drip down. Again, he turned and looked.

“If you just come down, you and your wife can discuss whatever needs to be discussed,” Elena said.

He was silent for a few minutes before adjusting his footing.

“Alright,” he said nervously. “But we’re leaving. We’re going to get our bags and we’re leaving this place.”

Elena nodded. “You can leave whenever you would like,” she said.

He slowly nodded. “Okay. I’m coming down.” He turned and started walking up the roof and behind the chimney.

Suddenly, he stumbled backwards and fell, rolling towards the edge. The crowd below gasped as he rolled over it and fell.

Alan and Reena watched as he hit the ground with a loud thud.

“I’m a nurse!” she screamed, running to him.

He was laying on his side with the back of his head crushed open and his neck disjointed. There was a large pool of blood flowing from his skull, and she noticed bone fragments in it. On his forehead was a large circular hole. Whatever had caused the hole had hit with enough force to push a bit of his skull inwards.

Alan walked up behind her and kneeled down, hovering over John as he coughed and some blood ran from his mouth.

Elena and another employee ran towards them and pushed them out of the way. They reached down and grabbed John's arms.

Reena protested as they started to pull him down the grass. "He's alive! Stop moving him!"

They didn't listen and made their way through the entrance gate and across the road, stopping beneath some trees that grew out of the dirt.

"That's good enough," Elena said to the employee as Alan and Reena ran to them.

"You shouldn't have moved him!" Reena said angrily, kneeling beside him.

He coughed once more, sending blood into the air, and then stopped moving. She felt for a pulse on his wrist and then moved her hand to his jaw, feeling again for a moment.

"He's dead." She stood. "You shouldn't have moved him."

She knew that he would have died anyways, but she was disgusted by their actions to get him across the road.

"I'm sorry," Elena said. "We will notify the authorities and take care of it." She turned to the crowd that had formed. "If everyone could please return to your day, it would be very much appreciated," she said, pointing to the stairs that led back to the hotel.

"No!" a man shouted defiantly.

"Please," Elena pleaded. A group of employees began gathering behind the crowd. "If anyone would like to speak to the police once they've arrived, we'll take your name and let the officers know." She looked to an employee who produced a notepad. "This man will take your name."

Several guests spoke to one another and then gave their names to the employee.

"Thank you," Elena said. She turned to Alan and Reena. "Please. We will take care of this. He will take your name if you want."

They looked back at the body and then at one another.

"What about Lily?" Alan asked.

"We will also have the police look over that," Elena said.

Reena was shaken and her legs felt weak. Her face had become pale and she felt nauseated. "Can we go?" she asked Alan.

He gripped her arm and held her steady. "Of course," he said.

They stepped away and made their way to the hotel.

"Where is Lily?" Reena asked him they made their way up the final few steps to the entrance. "He was so adamant that something happened to her."

Alan shrugged. "What about their kids? Who's going to tell them?" He felt his chest tighten and was overcome with sadness.

Hugh walked past them to Elena. He touched her hands gently.

"He was hit with something as he was walking up the roof," Reena said as she stuck her fork into her salad.

"I agree with you," Alan said, sliding his burger away and reaching for his beer.

"Who hit him?" she asked, looking around the dining room.

He shook his head. "Why did they hit him?" he asked.

She looked at him. "Let's go to the roof and see if there's anything up there."

He frowned. "What if we get caught?" he said, scanning the room to see if anyone was listening.

"We won't," she said, sounding confident.

He shook his head. "Let's wait until dark," he said, standing with her. "It would be better to go up there when no one on the ground can see."

They exited the dining hall and went to their room until nightfall.

At eleven-thirty, they quietly slipped out of their room, scanning the hallway to make sure no one was around.

They made their way to the side stairwell and proceeded up until they came to a large metal door that read "Employees Only". On the ground beside the door was the remnants of a chain, which had been cut and thrown down.

"I wonder if John did that?" Reena said as she reached for the handle and turned it, slightly tugging to pull it open. There was the shrill sound of metal grinding as the door slid against its frame.

"Shhhh!" Alan said, looking down the stairwell.

"I'm trying!" she said, shooting him an angry look.

The door opened and a rush of air filled the stairwell, rattling the descending doors that led to the other floors.

Reena stepped through first and found her footing on the thin metal stairs that led up to the roof. He followed and let the door close shut behind him. The same grinding noise filled the stairwell and echoed down.

"Shhhh!" she said.

"Be quiet," he said, gently pushing her up the stairs.

On the top of the roof, they could see far out. The ocean was visible under the moonlight, and to their far left there was a stretch of barren land that stretched as far as they could see.

They looked at the ground and allowed their gaze to follow the roadway that stretched in front of the hotel. They noticed an employee standing at the gates, and as they looked further, they could see more of them. Their flashlights illuminated a small path in front as they slowly walked back and forth along the road.

"What are they doing?" Alan asked.

"It's like they're patrolling," Reena said, walking to the spot where John had disappeared before rolling backwards and off the roof. She crouched down to get a better look and noticed something.

Alan followed and stood by the chimney, grasping it as the wind picked up, blowing across the roof and causing the trees to rustle.

"Look at this," she said, pointing.

"What is it?"

"It's blood spatter," she said, following the spots and lines of blood that crept their way across the roof and onto the bottom part of the chimney. "He was hit with something," she said, examining it more closely. "He was hit hard."

"How do you know that?" he asked her.

"Do you see this?" she said, pointing to a spatter of blood on the bottom of the chimney.

He nodded.

"It means that he was hit with enough force to cause the blood to travel and splatter like this," she said as she stood up.

"What do you think he was hit with?" he asked.

"A hammer." Reena stepped back to look at the entire area. "Someone wanted to make sure he didn't make it off this roof."

As they turned to leave, Alan noticed far away, beyond the forested area, right in the spot that he thought the cleared-out pit would be, a massive fire was burning. Its flames lit up the surrounding trees just enough to see, and the smoke rose high into the night sky, blending into the darkness and disappearing.

Reena saw it too. "What are they burning?"

He shook his head in silence. "What did they do with John's body?" he asked, watching the flames maintain their steady height and their strong illumination.

8

Alan and Reena were sitting quietly, eating breakfast together and each thinking about the previous day. Their Italian meal was good, but neither had a strong appetite and the food went cold long before they decided they were done.

Hugh exited the kitchen and proceeded to walk to the few tables where guests sat, spending a few moments with each before making his way to them.

"Good morning," he said, fixing his dark purple tie. "My name is Hugh, and I'm the manager of the hotel." He extended his hand towards Alan for him to shake. The hand was cold and solid, and Alan pulled back quickly.

"We would like to apologize for the situation that occurred yesterday, and as a good gesture, we are refunding the total for yesterday's fees." He pulled a check from his pocket and handed it to Alan. "Please, enjoy the rest of your stay," he said and walked away.

Alan set the check on the table and picked up his glass of water, taking a sip.

"I suppose it's something," Reena said as she watched Hugh disappear back into the kitchen. "Even if it's an empty gesture."

Alan set his glass down. "Do you want to go to Sun Garden in a bit and tour around? We could stop for lunch at the restaurant, too."

She smiled. "That's a nice idea."

He leaned back. "I want to get in a swim before we go though. Gimme an hour," he said, stretching his arms and legs and sliding his chair back.

While Alan went down to the pool, Reena rolled over onto the bed and dug her head into the pillow, sighing in relaxation. It was cool on her skin and she was thinking about their lovemaking session a few nights earlier, smiling as she stroked his side of the bed.

"We should have come to this resort," Reena said.

He nodded. "At least this one has other people in it…and no deaths."

She gave a half smile.

"Here you guys go," Victoria said as she set the coffees in front of them. "I'll come back in a few minutes and take your order." She stuck the tray under her arm and quickly walked away.

"I like her," Reena said, watching Victoria. She moved in and out of the tables with ease, greeting customers with a bright smile.

Alan was far off in another world, rubbing his thumb along the outside of his coffee cup.

"What are you thinking about?" Reena asked him.

He looked up at her and then down again. "Have you noticed that our hotel always seems smothering? Like there's a pressure inside?"

She wondered for a moment. "In some ways, I guess I have," she said, thinking to herself how his personality had taken a bit of an unexpected turn lately.

"I feel something there sometimes. It's like a darkness that starts in my legs and works itself up," he said. "And I can feel my mood slipping sometimes. I can feel an irritability starting."

"How come you didn't mention it before?" she asked.

"I didn't want to seem like I was overreacting," he said.

"Well, it is a different atmosphere at the hotel, and there's been a lot of strange things going on. John's fall didn't help," she said, brushing his hand with hers.

"It's probably nothing," he said, looking up as Victoria returned, pulling out her pad of paper.

"Alright," she said, clicking her pen. "What can I get for you today?"

After they ate, Victoria came by to collect the plates and they noticed she had her apron around her arm.

"All done for the day?" Reena asked.

"Yes," she said. "I'm just helping to clear my tables before I go home and relax."

Alan turned to Reena and then back to Victoria. "Do you want to join us for a coffee?" he asked, motioning to a chair beside Reena.

She thought for a moment. "Sure!" she said and disappeared to the kitchen with the plates in her hand.

She returned a few minutes later with a fresh pot of coffee and an empty cup. She slid out the chair and sat down, letting a sigh escape her lungs.

The three of them talked for a while, getting to know each other. Victoria was from San Diego and vacationed in Sun Garden for a month in the summer. She worked at the café, which was owned by her uncle.

"It's not too bad," she said. "He lets me stay in his spare bedroom and I get to spend a month here."

Reena sipped her coffee. "When do you leave?"

"In two days, actually," she said.

Alan frowned. "That's too bad. We're here for another four days. Do you want to stay until then?" he joked.

Victoria gave a small laugh. "No, I think I'll head back in two days. This area gets a little weird after a while." She glanced out the window.

"Weird?" Reena asked.

"Yeah. Becomes unsettling. Where are you two staying?" she asked.

"At the Laelynn," Alan said, flicking his eyes to Reena.

"And you haven't noticed how weird it gets?" Victoria asked, a surprised expression on her face. "Nothing strange at all?"

He thought for a moment. "There's been a few things," he said, looking to Reena.

"One of the other guests killed himself yesterday," she said, shuffling in her seat. "He jumped from the roof."

"Are you sure he killed himself?" Victoria asked.

"Well," Reena said, pausing, "we think he was murdered."

Victoria laughed amusingly. "You don't have to think it! If what everyone hears about the Laelynn is true, he was definitely murdered."

Alan leaned forward. "What do they say?"

She sat back. "They say that a cult runs it, that it's haunted, that there's lots of people who go there and never leave. They're never seen again."

He laughed. "That all sounds a bit superstitious."

Reena opened her mouth to speak but stopped.

"What is it?" Victoria asked.

"What about Lily?" she asked Alan. "John said she was missing."

"Who's Lily?" Victoria asked, taking a sip of her coffee.

"The man who killed himself yesterday, Lily was his wife. He said how she went missing and he was scared," Reena said, crossing her arms.

Victoria paused for a moment. "You see? Isn't that strange that a man became so upset that he climbed to the roof and apparently jumped because he couldn't find his wife?"

Reena focused on a woman across from them. She appeared to be watching their conversation.

Alan rested on his elbows. "It is, yeah, but we really don't know what his mental state was. Maybe he had some issues and that was logical to him."

"Logic goes out the window when the Laelynn is involved," Victoria said. "All I know is what I hear, and I've heard that place is dangerous."

Reena turned to her. "Can you elaborate?"

Victoria looked at her watch. "I have five minutes until my uncle gets here" she said, nodding. "So, the hotel was built in the nineteen thirties by a man named Arthur Laelynn. He was a very religious man, and it's said that he created a religious movement in the hotel. He was nice, they say. Anyways, his wife, Helen, gave birth to two sons; Robert in nineteen forty-six and Charles in nineteen forty-eight." She paused and took a sip of her coffee.

"Now, here's where it gets weird. Around nineteen fifty-eight, Arthur's wife was found dead on the beach, just off the property, and they never found her killer. In nineteen sixty-six, Arthur himself was murdered. Again, he was found dead on the beach, no suspects."

Alan and Reena leaned forward.

"Shortly after Arthur went missing, Charles was found hanging from a tree across from the hotel. It was ruled as suicide and then forgotten about."

"And what about Robert?" Alan asked.

"I'm getting there," Victoria said. "After Arthur went missing, the property and his estate passed to Robert. The religious followers that Arthur established were also inherited by him. This is where the rumor of a cult comes from. People began disappearing once they went to the hotel, and Robert started sending security to patrol the perimeter of the property."

Reena continued watching the woman across from them. She moved in her chair and glanced their direction.

"But what happened to him?" Alan asked, resting his chin on his hand.

"No one knows. In nineteen ninety-seven, he just disappeared. The police did a small investigation, questioning Hugh and everyone else. Nothing ever came up," Victoria said. "Is Hugh still there?"

They nodded.

"He'll be there until he disappears too. I'm telling you, that place is dangerous."

She stood to leave.

"I hate to leave you with that, but I have to get going," she said. "I hope I'll see you guys again before I leave. If not, though, take care!"

When she was gone, Alan and Reena sighed.

"Do you believe her?" he asked.

"I believe that there's something strange about that place," she said as she stood.

"Where are you going?" he asked, standing with her.

"We're going for a walk. Since we got here, there's been a woman at the table over there who's been watching the entire time," she whispered.

He turned and looked behind him, trying to see who she was motioning to.

"Who?" he asked her as they walked towards the door. "I can't see who you're talking about."

"Come on," she said, stepping out of the restaurant and onto the sidewalk.

They quickly crossed the street and passed a few stores, slipping into the nearest giftshop.

"Let's watch for a second," Reena said. They stood in the window, hiding themselves behind a rack of clothing.

Within a few minutes, a woman stepped out of the restaurant and onto the sidewalk, looking up and down the street. She walked down a couple of stores and stopped, shading her face with her hand and looking behind her.

"You see," Reena said, nudging his shoulder.

"But who is she?" Alan asked.

Around the corner of the street, running towards the mystery woman from the restaurant, came Elena. She approached the woman and they exchanged some words, their faces screwed up in confusion. They were looking for someone.

9

Arthur stood, gazing up at the massive building that had just been built. The gardens surrounding it were full of life. The flower beds were several feet deep, and the spectrum of colours from each flower danced as the breeze blew across them.

"It's magnificent!" Helen said, grasping his hand.

"It is, isn't it?" he said, turning towards her and kissing her cheek. "It'll be the perfect place for us to create our family and our life."

"Excuse me," a man said from behind them.

They turned. "Would you like us to start moving your things into your suite?" he asked.

Arthur nodded and the man crossed the road to a house. They had lived in the house a number of years while the building was being built, waiting to move in. It was small and built in nineteen twelve. He was born in the area after his parents relocated to take part in the expanding silver mining operations.

Arthur was a religious man, having been raised by his parents to strictly follow the Bible. Severe punishment was instilled whenever a deviation occurred, and he could vividly remember having to recite passages for hours while professing his sins in a dark, cold room that his father set up specifically to cleanse his soul. After he was done his confessions, depending on how genuine his father felt he had been, flogging was common. He would be forced to flog himself. If he didn't do it good enough, his father would step in and finish. Arthur had deep scars along his back as a reminder.

After his parent's deaths in eighteen ninety-nine, he started to view religion as open ended, and began believing that he was a messenger of God. He slowly built a following of men, women, and children, who, like him, believed their religious ideals could be more. Over the course of a few years, their beliefs began to merge into one. They prayed three times daily, and welcomed anyone into their group; homosexuals, different nationalities, and any gender was treated with the same respect.   Eventually, they referred to themselves as Heaven United, believing that Arthur was their sacred messenger, idolizing him.

In nineteen twenty-five, Helen joined the group and they quickly fell in love. Soon after, they married.

The inheritance from his parents' deaths included a portion of land, and he built the small house on it. A few years after marrying Helen, the group had grown to over one hundred fifty members, too large to continue teaching on the grounds of the house. Arthur and Helen began looking for new land to build on. They found an area large enough just down from their house, and quickly bought it.

The first brick was laid in nineteen thirty-one. Arthur funded the entire project and Helen planned every detail. It was their perfect oasis. In nineteen thirty-five, it was officially done and ready to be inhabited.

They watched as a group of men began moving their things out of the house, carrying them across the roadway and up the steps of the building.

"When is everyone expected?" Arthur asked Helen.

"Tomorrow evening at six," she said as they walked up the steps and made their way inside. "Everything will be ready."

They had announced an official unveiling to their followers and were throwing a dinner party. The building consisted of three hundred rooms, and all the members were encouraged to move in. It was a daunting task which would begin the day following their dinner, so they had hired a group of local men to ease the process.

"It's all coming together beautifully," Helen said as she opened the windows in their room and breathed in the fresh ocean mist mixed with the smell of the new paint.

After years of waiting, their vision was starting to move forward.

The evening of the dinner party, the dining room was completely full. Everyone mingled and laughter filled the air.

Arthur walked to a make-shift podium and greeted the crowd.

"Welcome to the Laelynn!" he said enthusiastically, raising his hands in the air.

The crowd applauded and some cheered, screaming above the clapping.

"My wife and I are so happy that everyone could join us, and we hope that everyone has chosen to stay and live here," he said to another round of cheering. "All of your personal belongings should now be in your rooms, and we encourage you to make yourselves at home. After all, this is your home now. We are all a family." He clasped his hands together. "Everyone should have found pins on their dressers, and we ask that you wear them at all times as a symbol of faith."

The crowd cheered, and some touched their chests, feeling the pins under their fingers.

He motioned for Helen to join him and she stood up, leaning over to the microphone.

"We couldn't be happier that everyone is here, and now we can move forward with our faith, finally together forever. God bless Heaven United!"

Another round of cheering followed as Arthur and Helen stepped down from the podium and disappeared into the crowd, spending the rest of the evening visiting with their followers.

As the years went by, the group slowly grew and their faith remained strong. Arthur and Helen were kind and generous leaders, and the idolization that they were shown only increased.

In the spring of nineteen forty-six, Helen gave birth to a son, Robert. The birth was a celebration unlike anything she expected. The followers gave gifts and flowers to the new parents. Hours were spent passing the baby around between rooms, each follower saying prayers and messages to God while holding the baby.

A month passed and the celebration slowly began to fade, allowing Arthur and Helen time to breathe and relax, finally finding time to appreciate their new son.

"He's beautiful," Helen would say, rocking him back and forth, his cooing soothing her.

Two years later, another son was born; Charles, and another month-long celebration followed before slowly subsiding. Their family was now complete.

When Robert turned ten, things slowly changed. Arthur and Helen began noticing subtle changes in him, and they gradually became increasingly alarming.

He had taken to physically abusing Charles; scratching, punching, and kicking him so that he was either bleeding or limping. One day, he pushed him down a flight of stairs and broke his arm.

"Why did you do that?" Helen screamed as she grabbed Robert and pulled him away from Charles.

He shrugged, not seeming to care.

She slapped his face and pulled at his arm as one of the followers brought Charles into the room and sat him on the bed.

"I'll be right back." She picked Robert up and carried him down the hallway to Arthur's study.

Another slap followed, this time from Arthur, before he was forced to pray and ask for forgiveness. He sat on his knees, his hands clasped, staring with blank eyes at the crucifix before him.

Robert felt the eerie figure of Jesus was looking into his soul.

"Forgive me," he said as he clenched his teeth and stared forward. His thoughts, breaking from forgiveness, flashed through images of dead animals, dead bodies, and on the cross, his father, crucified and with nails through his hands, hanging as he slowly died. A grin formed on Robert's face as he stood up, threw the rosary to the bottom of the cross, and exited the room.

Robert became fascinated with death and began torturing animals. One day, he found a German Shepherd. It adored his affection and followed him around. He took it behind the building and into a secluded area. He sat on the dog to keep it from moving and pulled out a large kitchen knife from his jacket. He petted its head, relaxing it, and then pushed the knife far into its neck. The dog kicked and cried out, trying to get out from under Robert's weight, before it slowly died.

He took the body to a small grave he'd dug and threw it in,

dropping the knife on top. He looked in for a moment, and then started burying it. As he turned and started to walk back to the front of the building, he caught a glimpse of Charles, looking out a window towards him.

He stopped and stared at him, noticing his face was pale and frozen. *He saw*, he thought to himself as he began running to the front of the building, then up the stairs and to the room Charles was in.

He burst through the door as Charles jumped on his bed and hid his face.

"Did you see?!" he yelled, climbing on top of him. He pushed Charles's cast arm aside. "Did you?!"

Charles was shaking, tears forming in his eyes. "No!" he screamed.

"You did, didn't you?" Robert asked him, holding him down.

"No! I didn't see anything!"

Robert noticed blood on his jacket and rubbed it, then placed his hand on Charles' face, smearing the blood over it.

"If you say anything, I'll kill you." He stood up, forcefully pushing on Charles's stomach as he did so. "I'll bury you with the dog, and no one will ever wonder what happened to you. No one cares, and they won't look for you. You keep your fucking mouth shut."

Charles didn't move, looking at him with terrified eyes.

"Go wash that shit off your face," Robert said as he turned and opened the door.

He slammed the door and left Charles on the bed, crying and rubbing his face.

A week after killing the dog, Robert was walking through the hallways when he thought he saw something. He followed it, hurrying to catch up but seeming to lose it.

He broke into a run and dashed around a corner, suddenly stopping and freezing in one spot. In front of him, growling, was the dog he had stabbed, the wound from the knife visible.

"It can't be," he said to himself as he stepped closer to the dog. "I killed you."

It stepped back and turned around, starting to run as Robert went after it. It bolted around another corner and he followed, stopping once he came to a dead end. The dog had disappeared, vanishing with nowhere to go.

"A ghost," he said to himself as he stared into the dead end, wondering to himself whether or not that was possible.

A few days later, he decided to test this thought and found a cat with white and brown fur. It wouldn't allow him to pick it up, so he cornered it and picked up a large rock. The cat hissed and growled, arching its back as he threw the rock at its head. It fell and stopped moving. He stepped closer and kicked it, waiting for any movement. Nothing. He lifted it up by its front legs and examined the caved-in skull.

He carried the cat behind the building and buried it.

A week later, he toured the property for hours, walking the floors several times, waiting to see the cat. The sun had almost set and he was about to give up his search when he noticed something in one of the gardens outside, sitting in the shade of the trees.

A white and brown cat with a partially dented skull, licking its paws and giving itself a bath.

"Hi," he said as he bent down and watched it.

One of the followers passed away in their room from a heart attack a year after his experiments with the animals, and for weeks he expected to see her ghost roaming around. It never manifested, and he wondered that if it wasn't a violent death, maybe their soul moved on.

One day in the summer of nineteen fifty-eight, Helen was taking a walk on the beach, relaxing after a lengthy sermon. Arthur was aware she was gone, and the kids remained in their rooms.

"Where's mother?" Robert asked Arthur as he followed him to his bedroom.

"She's at the beach," he said, laying down on his bed. "I'm going to have a nap. You be good and stay in the hotel." He closed his eyes as Robert left the room and shut the door.

Robert waited a few minutes and then checked on Charles, who was quietly playing in his room. He stepped in and startled him.

"Stay in here and don't come out." He shut the door firmly and skipped down the stairs to the front door.

Helen was laying on a towel, her eyes closed and her thoughts far away.

Behind her, Robert crept slowly along the rocks to the sand. His feet were silent, and his small hand clutched a large rock.

She breathed in and sighed, listening to the waves as they splashed their way onto the beach.

Excruciating pain exploded in her head and she reached behind her as darkness grasped her vision. She screamed and felt the warmth of blood as it flowed from her forehead.

Robert threw his hand back again and brought it down, hitting her on the same spot. Again and again he repeated the act until he exhausted himself and dropped the rock.

In front of him, his mother's body lay, motionless. He sat on the sand and looked out over the ocean. His arm ached and he rubbed it for a while before standing and picking the rock up. He walked towards the water and threw it in, then bent down and rinsed his hands off.

He walked past Helen's body, not stopping to see his work, and continued. He made his way up the steps, went to his room, laid on the bed and fell asleep.

It was dark outside when one of the maids burst into the room and woke him. Charles was with her.

"Please, come quick!" the woman said to him as she turned and grabbed Charles's arm. "Something has happened and your father needs you."

They made their way to Arthur's study and saw him leaning on his desk, praying loudly. As they sat on the couch across from him, he looked up, and through watery eyes, said, "Your mother is dead."

Charles began sobbing, rubbing his eyes.

"What happened?" Robert asked, trying to seem as upset as possible.

Arthur explained what they found and told the kids to not leave until the murderer was found. They agreed, and after mourning together as a family, they all slept in Arthur's bedroom. Robert and Charles were in the bed, and Arthur slept on the floor.

Robert lay awake, staring at the ceiling, his thoughts occupied by the image of what he had done.

In nineteen sixty-six, eight years after Helen's murder, Arthur had finally found peace with what had occurred. After a year of keeping the kids close and not allowing them to venture outside alone, he relaxed and gave them their freedom back. He reasoned that the killer had been passing through, took advantage of the situation and then fled long ago.

After initially suspecting many members of the group, he found it within himself, with the help of his faith, to forgive any wrongdoing that may have occurred and returned to his position as the leader.

"Why have you forgiven her death?" Robert asked.

"Because, son, God forgives all," Arthur said. "If we trust in God, we can trust in anyone."

Every year, during the anniversary of her death, Arthur would return to the spot they had found her to leave a small bouquet of flowers and say a prayer.

This year, he returned to the spot and sat down. He began talking to her, knowing that she was listening from somewhere.

"Charles is doing good," he said as he tossed some small pebbles into the water. "He's almost eighteen and Robert just turned twenty, but you know that."

The waves crashed hard as the wind picked up.

"I'm nervous for Robert to eventually take over," he said. "Charles would be a better choice. I feel he's ready for it. I wish you were here to help me with this."

The sound of the waves muffled Robert's steps as he approached, the gun in his hand aimed at Arthur's head.

"Goodbye, father," he said as he pulled the trigger and a loud bang echoed over the beach and across the water.

Arthur's head jolted to the side and he collapsed on the sand.

Robert walked to the water and pulled his arm back, releasing all the energy he had and throwing the gun as far out as he could.

He turned and walked past Arthur's body, glancing to it as he made his way up the bank and left.

After the shock of Arthur's death had spread through the group, a mixture of sympathy and suspicion settled on the brothers. Robert had even heard whisperings that some members suspected that they were responsible for Helen's death as well.

A few months passed and the group was becoming increasingly unsettled. Several members had left, and more were considering it.

The donations that used to steadily flow in were slipping, as was the respect and admiration that was once felt.

One night, he woke Charles up.

"Come with me," he said, shaking him. "I heard a bang outside, like an explosion."

Charles sat up in bed, squinting in the darkness. "An explosion?"

"Yes," Robert said. "I need your help to see what it was."

"Where are we going," Charles asked as he was forcibly shoved through the doorway of his room.

"Are you questioning me?" Robert asked him, placing his hand on his shoulder.

"No, I'm sorry," he said, moving forward and down the stairs. "It's just so late."

Robert shoved him. "Quit talking."

As they made their way outside, he pointed across the road and to a large set of trees that rose out from the barren dirt and pushed Charles towards them.

"You see," he said as he stood behind him, pointing underneath the trees to a chair with a coiled-up piece of rope on it.

Charles squinted his eyes to see when suddenly, Robert swung his arm around his neck and squeezed, cutting off his airway. He clawed at his brother's arms, trying to fight the grip off.

"Stop moving," Robert whispered into his ear. "Let go!"

He lost consciousness and slumped to the ground. Robert bent down and felt for a pulse. It was weak, but he was alive.

He grabbed his arms and pulled him underneath one of the trees, then let him slump back down.

He walked to the chair and slid it under the tree, then quickly fastened a noose. He placed it around Charles's neck, tightening it, and then tossed the other end up and over a sturdy branch.

"Goodbye, Charles," he said as he turned and grabbed the loose end of the rope and walked further back, slowly hoisting Charles's body off the ground.

He stood and watched his brother swinging for a few minutes before placing the chair underneath his hanging legs and kicking it over. He reached into his pocket and removed a folded-up note. He opened it and read it.

I'm sorry for what I've done. I can't explain my actions, but I hope for forgiveness. My mother and father didn't deserve what I did, and I can't live with my actions any longer. Forgive me, Lord, and allow my entrance into Heaven.'

He tucked the note into Charles's pocket and stepped back. The creaking of the rope slowed as Robert made his way back inside.

A month after Charles was found and blamed for the deaths of Arthur and Helen, Robert was showered with sympathy, and the respect that had been lost came back. He was their leader, their saviour, and their current messenger from God.

Over a period of a year, he found several group members that didn't share the same admiration he felt he deserved, and they were dealt with. They would be taken across the road, off the property, to the small house that his parents had lived in years before, and executed. It was through intimidation that he found members willing to murder, and once the executions were completed, the bodies were taken to the very back of the property, thrown in a pit, burned, and then buried.

The group slowly decreased in number, but those that did remain were fiercely loyal to him. He knew that power only existed when there were people to pray on, and he decided to open the building to tourists who were coming to the area; creating a resort, of sorts, and advertising it as the perfect vacation spot. The remaining group members worked, inconspicuously, to convert the tourists to their group, and if this failed, they were killed, burned, and buried. If the tourists were reported missing, the group worked hard to create a story that the guest had checked out of the hotel and carried on with their vacation.

A patrol was set up to keep the property secure. They were placed at the entrance of the hotel and down the roadway that stretched to the beach.

Years later, in nineteen seventy-eight, Robert became a father to a son, Hugh. Before Hugh, there had been three daughters; rape children. He had envisioned passing the group to a son, and when each of the girls were born, they were quickly disposed of.

As Hugh grew older, he was instilled with his father's ideas and groomed to be a good replacement. All of his malice was poured into Hugh, and a violent personality was encouraged.

In nineteen ninety-seven, at the age of fifty-one, Robert began feeling ill. After learning that it was cancer, he started to think of the dog and cat he still saw regularly and wondered if he could continue as a ghost within the hotel, forever being part of it.

But another thought occurred to him. Through the proper vessel, he wondered if he could take his ghost self beyond the borders of the property and out into the world.

A month later, feeling particularly weak and worn down, he entered his study in the hotel and admired the flowers illuminated by the candlelight around the room. He walked to his bed and sat down as a follower brought him his Bible. He took it and lay down, covering his legs up as he was handed two cyanide pills.

He put them in his mouth and bit down, grimacing at the sensation. It slowly faded, and as he closed his eyes, he told the men to leave.

A dizziness began to engulf him, and his final thought focused on the significance of his return.

Three months after his death, the sadness the group felt started to dissipate. Hugh took over his father's position, and everything was returning to how it previously was.

One evening as Hugh turned off his bedside lamp and closed his eyes to sleep, he felt a sudden chill come across him.

He turned in bed, trying not to wake his wife, Elena, and set his feet on the floor. He stood and stared into the darkness that shrouded the furthest part of the room.

"I know you're there," he said quietly, hearing himself breathing.

The moonlight illuminated half of the room, and the half that remained black seemed to shake with restlessness.

"I've been waiting for you," he said as he stepped towards the darkness.

A black hand, partially decayed, emerged and moved towards him. The hand became an arm, and then a body stood out, vaguely resembling the shape of a human.

Its white eyes focused on Hugh. They were lidless and without pupils, and as he felt them pierce through his soul, he knew it was his father.

"You look different," he said as the figure came closer.

The figure didn't speak as it brought its hands up and rested them on either side of Hugh's head. Images began flickering through his mind.

His father, dying, floating through darkness. Then a flash that showed him laying on his back, his body starting to break down and rot; turning a dark grey, then brown, and finally black. The body sat up, and then stood. It looked up, and instantly, Hugh was back in the room.

He stood for a moment, feeling a heaviness in his chest. "I've missed you," he said to the figure.

It nodded.

"Soon," Hugh said, "you will be outside of these walls, free to do whatever you want, and no earthly being can stop you."

The figure stepped back and disappeared into the darkness.

Hugh walked to his lamp and clicked it on. The figure was gone, but the chill in the air remained.

10

Alan and Reena stared at the ceiling, blinking in silence as the wind outside blew against their window. The morning sun was shining and the clock read seven.

Again, a loud knock came from the door and Alan stepped out of bed and put his shorts on.

"Yes?" he said as he opened the door, impatience in his voice.

"I'm sorry," Elena said. She looked at his shirtless chest and then peered behind him to their bed.

"It's early," he said, stepping to the side to block her view of Reena. They hadn't seen Elena since the day outside the restaurant.

"We were just doing a welfare check on you two to make sure everything was alright," she said.

He frowned. "A welfare check? Why would you need to do that?"

"May I come in?" she asked as she stepped towards the opening beside him.

He blocked her way. "No, I don't think so. It's early and we're not ready. What do you need, Elena?" he asked, frustrated.

"After what happened to John, we were concerned for the guests, and then you two left and went to Sun Garden. We were just hoping you were alright."

Reena walked up behind him and stood in the opening. "We're fine, Elena. Please, could you go?"

Elena shuffled and stepped back.

"If you say you're alright, then yes, I will." She glanced over her shoulder as she walked away and then disappeared into the stairwell.

"That's odd," Alan said as he shut the door and climbed into bed.

"She's full of shit," Reena said as she joined him. "She was looking for us for another reason."

Alan nodded. "I know," he said as he grasped her body. "Ignore her," he mumbled, and they both fell asleep.

It was noon when they woke up, starving, and decided to have a quick lunch and then head to the beach.

Downstairs, all the tables were empty.

Luis walked out of the kitchen and started removing the empty buffet trays, seeming to use extra caution to not drop any. He saw them at their table and nodded.

"Good afternoon," Alan said, waving.

"Hola." He went to the kitchen and returned with a washcloth. "I didn't see you for breakfast," he said, starting to wipe one of the buffet tables.

"We slept in," Reena said as she sipped her coffee. "Elena woke us up at seven."

Luis frowned and looked at the entrance of the kitchen, then walked towards them.

"I hope you told her to fuck off," he whispered, laughing to himself.

Reena choked on her sandwich. "Yes," she laughed. "That's the first time I've heard you swear."

Luis rolled his eyes. "I feel exhausted today," he said, trying to stifle a yawn. "Maybe that's why."

Alan set his cup down. "Didn't get a good sleep?"

"No," Luis said, "there was an emergency staff meeti -" He stopped himself.

"A staff meeting?" Reena asked as she wiped her hands on her napkin.

"Well, yes," Luis said, stumbling over his words. "Sort of, I guess you could say."

"About what?" Reena asked.

Luis stared for a moment and then looked at the kitchen, hearing muffled voices. "Company rules," he said, vaguely, and walked back to the buffet table. He began wiping quickly as Elena and Hugh came out of the kitchen and towards him.

They spoke with one another, too quietly for Alan and Reena to hear. Hugh shook his finger at Luis as Elena shook her head.

After a few minutes, they left and he resumed cleaning.

Alan and Reena walked to him, and as they approached, he looked at them.

"I can't be seen talking to you," he said. "I've done a few things wrong and I'm being…watched."

"You always seem to be in trouble," Reena said as she eyed the kitchen entrance, "but I never see you doing anything wrong."

Alan nodded.

"I'm always doing something wrong, according to him," Luis said, anger filling his voice. "But please, go. I really can't be caught talking to you."

They hesitated and then left, feeling sorry for him.

The sun was baring down as they swam in the water, splashing one another and laughing like children.

"Will you miss it here?" Alan asked her.

She bobbed up and down, thinking. "I'm excited to get home and do those renovations."

He rolled his eyes. "I forgot all about those," he said, splashing her face.

"I didn't," she said, disappearing under the water.

She swam underneath him and yanked off his swimming trunks.

He screamed and reached down as she popped up in front of him, holding the shorts in the air.

"Give them back!" he said, lunging towards her. "I could untie this," he said as his hands grasped the bow that kept her bikini top on.

"Don't you dare," she said, handing the shorts back.

"I wouldn't mind it," he joked as he pulled his hands back.

"They would," she said, pointing to a few kids who had come from the direction of Sun Garden.

"Where is the adults only section?" he joked, reaching down and putting his shorts back on.

"It's in the bedroom," Reena said as she swam closer to the beach and walked out of the water.

He followed and laid on the towel that was spread out.

"Well, I'll miss it here," he said, rolling onto his stomach and resting his chin on his hand.

"How come?" she asked as she laid down beside him.

"Because it's been nice just being with you. There's been no one else to distract me from you."

She smiled. "I'll miss that too."

They laid in the sun together for a few hours, relaxing, hands wandered around each other's bodies.

"Let's go back to the hotel," Reena said and stood. "I don't want to get charged for indecency."

Alan laughed and jumped up, grabbing the towel. He handed it to Reena and she wrapped it around herself, forming an ill-fitting dress.

They made their way back, passing several employees who wandered the road that led to the hotel.

Once they were inside, they made their way up to their room, undressing as the door shut.

Breathing heavily, they both fell into bed and worked their way up into it. The sand from their bodies coated the bed and the bit of sweat on them was quickly absorbed by the sheets.

A severe chill filled the room, removing any warmth that had been lingering. The wall moved slightly; a wave seemed to emanate from somewhere behind the wallpaper to slowly move across it.

Reena bit down hard on his lip, a metallic taste filling her mouth.

"Ouch!" he exclaimed, pushing her away as he reached up to it and felt. A small spot of blood was on his fingertips. "Be careful," he said, staring at her. She suddenly looked different. There was an animalistic glint in her eyes.

She leaned forward to kiss him again but he hesitated.

"Jesus," she said, "don't be such a baby."

A shock crossed his face and he pushed her further away. This wasn't Reena.

"Let's stop," he said as he started to slide off the bed.

She grabbed at his arm and tightened her grip. "No," she said, increasing her hold.

"Let go!" he demanded, pulling his arm forcibly away from her.

He jumped to his feet and walked around to her side, looking at her inquisitively. Something was off.

"Are you feeling okay?" he asked.

"I'm fine," she said. "Come back to bed…let's fuck."

He stepped back, feeling a sense of revulsion in his stomach. "Quit talking like that!"

She laughed as she slid her hand between her legs and held it there, massaging herself.

He stepped forward and grabbed it, pulling it away from what she was doing and using his other hand to cover her up.

"Stop that!" he said as she laid her head on the pillow, sighed, and slapped the blankets beside her in anger.

She stood from the bed and slid on her bikini bottoms, watching him as she did it with a piercing look in her eyes.

"Why did I agree to marry such a weak man?" she said as she walked to the door. She stopped abruptly and spun around, a look of sadness hitting her face.

"I didn't mean that," she said, bringing her hand to her mouth. "I didn't."

He looked at her in disappointment.

"I didn't mean that!" she said again, quickly running to him.

There was a sickness building in her stomach. She felt as though she was on the verge of throwing up.

"Why did I ask such a bitch to marry me?" he asked, striding past her towards the door.

She ran after him and grabbed his shoulders, spinning him around.

"Stop!" she yelled. "This isn't us!"

He hesitated and turned to the door. She forcibly grabbed him again, not noticing his hand coming towards her face. It struck with enough force to knock her off balance and she fell backwards, landing hard on the floor.

She laid there as he stepped closer and stopped, looking down at her.

"Don't touch me again," he said, raising his fist in the air.

He opened the door, pausing a moment before he left and slammed it loudly.

Reena sat on the ground, tears forming in her eyes and then falling down her face. He had never hit her before, and she never felt threatened by him in any way. She wondered if a side she had never known in him was coming out.

After calming down enough to leave the room, she looked around for Alan but didn't find him. She assumed he may have left the property and decided to do the same and walk to Sun Garden.

Outside, the sun was low in the sky, creating long shadows, and as she made her way to the restaurant, she hoped Victoria was working.

"Is Victoria here?" she asked the hostess at the front of the restaurant.

"She is," the woman said. "I'll go get her for you."

Reena sat for a few minutes and waited. She could still feel the stinging in her face from the slap, and her tailbone and spine ached. She thought to herself how she had acted differently, too. She said things to him that she normally wouldn't.

"Reena!" Victoria said as she came around the counter, smiling her bright smile.

Instantly, Victoria's smile faded as she looked at Reena's face and saw her reddened cheek and sad expression. She rushed to her and touched her face.

"What happened?" she asked as she ushered her to a private table in the back and sat down across from her. "I'm done my shift, let's talk."

As another waitress brought some coffee to their table and then left, Reena started telling her what happened.

"He hit me," she said, moving the spoon in her cup to dissolve the sugar.

"He hit you?!" Victoria asked, anger in her voice.

"He didn't mean it."

Victoria hesitantly nodded.

Reena told her what she had done as well, wiping the occasional tear that crept its way out of her eyes. "I felt like a different person," she said. "And he was a different person."

Victoria was frowning as she stared at the table.

"Look," she said, reaching for Reena's hand. "You need to get out. It's not safe. You need to go find Alan and get the hell out of there."

Reena looked at her, peering into her eyes, and knew she was right.

"If he's missing, it's not because he's hiding, it's because they've hidden him. You both are in danger," Victoria said as she slid her cup away from her, grabbed one of the napkins on the table, and reached into her purse with it. "Here," she said as she slid the napkin across the table towards Reena, hiding something in it.

She took it and opened the end. It was a gun.

"I carry one whenever I'm here. This place makes me feel uneasy, and it helps to make me feel a bit better. I'm leaving tomorrow, so it's yours now."

Reena began to protest and slid it back. "I don't need this," she said, almost on the verge of laughing. "I really don't. I'll go find him, we'll pack our bags, and we'll be gone tonight on the bus."

Victoria gave a half-hearted laugh and slid it back. "No, keep it. I don't know if you'll need it, but just take it."

Reena hesitated, feeling the metal beneath the paper napkin.

"Please," Victoria said.

Reena nodded slowly. "Alright," she said, sliding it across the table and into her purse. "I'll take it."

"Thank you," Victoria said as a waitress walked to their table.

"Victoria," she said, "your uncle is here."

Victoria looked at the front of the restaurant as a man waved to her. "Look, I have to go. My last day is tomorrow. Please get out of there, Reena. You need to go." She leaned towards Reena, giving a tight hug. "I'm so happy to have met you and Alan, and I hope everything works out. I pray it does."

Reena was slowly finishing her coffee when a sudden jolt of worry hit her.

She threw some money on the table and made her way back to the hotel.

Alan had searched for her, checking any area that he thought she may be. Now he was beginning to worry.

You hit her, he thought to himself. *You hit your wife, of course you can't find her.*

He entered their room and stood, looking around.

She needs time, he thought as he sat on their bed, remembering his actions. *She'll be back. Let her have the space she needs.*

His mind raced and he felt his concentration slipping.

"Go for a swim, collect yourself, and then try and find her," he said aloud as he stood and grabbed a clean pair of swimming shorts, slipped them on, and then left for the pool.

As he walked past the main desk, he saw Hugh and Elena discussing something through the window into the office. They stopped their conversation and both watched him, a menacing look across their faces.

Beyond that, he saw Luis and greeted him with a nod.

"Hola," Luis said as he walked to the office and shut the door behind himself.

Alan made his way to the pool room and opened the door, smelling the overwhelming scent of chlorine as he walked over the tiled floor to the deep end.

He jumped in and dove down, pausing underneath to hover in weightlessness for a minute before surfacing and letting himself float on the surface. He closed his eyes and thought about Reena.

The sound of cracking made him open his eyes and look around, the water splashing as he did so.

Again, a sound of cracking echoed through the room and off the walls, louder this time.

"Who's there?" He listened and then swam to the edge of the pool, looking around as he braced himself with his hand on the wall.

A few feet in front of him, the tiles on the floor had been moved. Several of them had been broken and pushed upwards.

He pulled himself out of the water and walked the few feet to them, crouching down to look. They had been pushed from underneath, it appeared, and buckled on top. He looked around and then back at them, noticing slight movement underneath.

He bent down closer and watched. A black finger made its way through the cracks, and he wondered if he was seeing things.

An arm protruded and shot upwards, then bent down and rested on the floor.

He jumped back and slipped on the tile, landing hard on his back. The air was knocked out of his lungs and he struggled to breathe.

Another arm reached out of the opening, and then gave way to a grotesque body that emerged and began crawling towards him.

Its arms reached out and grasped at his foot as he struggled to move backwards. The nails on the fingers brushed the sole of his foot and cut it open. Streaks of blood mixed with the pool water and created a swirling mixture of red on the white tile.

He screamed as the figure lurched forwards and grabbed his leg, its nails digging into the muscles, pulling him closer to it.

Kicking, he loosened its grip and slid backwards into the water while the figure grabbed the edge of the pool and crawled closer, peering down at him.

He swam underneath the water to the other end of the pool and surfaced, quickly grabbing for the edge while looking behind him. The figure stood up and watched.

He had no time to process the hand carrying a metal pipe that came down with quick speed and hit him across the forehead. Blood erupted and he sank back into the water, floating on the surface as the blood leeched into the pool.

Peering down into the water was Hugh, the metal pipe still securely in his hand. He turned and watched his father step backwards into the hole in the floor. The tile fixed itself and the floor became smooth as Hugh turned to Alan in the pool.

"I'll help you," Elena said as she came into the room and walked to him. "I never really liked him," she said. She reached one arm around and hugged Hugh.

11

"Where is my husband?!" Reena yelled, banging her fist on the counter.

"We're not sure," Elena said as she typed into her computer.

"Stop typing!" Reena said, her voice filled with anger. "Call the police so we can find him!"

Elena looked at her. "We have called the police," she said. "They'll be here as soon as they can be."

Reena stepped back from the desk and turned away. She could feel tears in her eyes and she didn't want to cry in front of Elena.

"I'll call the police myself," she said as she pulled out her cellphone and turned it on.

Elena looked at her. "That won't be necessary! As I've already told you, Hugh has notified the police and they'll be here as soon as they can be!"

Reena couldn't stop worrying about Alan and it was making her sick. This was the first major fight they had ever had, and the thought of not being able to see him was taking its toll on her.

The front door opened and a police officer came in.

Reena turned to Elena, who smiled at her. "I told you they would come as soon as possible."

The officer walked to the desk and spoke with Elena.

"This is his wife," Elena said, pointing to Reena.

He introduced himself to her. "I'm Officer Coello." He handed her a pad of paper and a pen. "Please, I need you to write down what happened in as much detail as possible."

Reena sat on the couch in the lobby and began writing; detailing the fight that had occurred, her walk to Sun Garden, and how when she returned she couldn't find Alan.

He took the notepad and then asked to see the pool room.

Inside, everything looked normal. Nothing had been changed from earlier.

They were about to leave when Reena saw several marks on the tile at the edge of the pool, just before it dropped down into the water. She bent down and looked at it closer. It was blood, and she frantically called Officer Coello over to her.

He examined it and took some photos with his phone, then dialed a number. "Hey, it's Isaac. I have a possible kidnapping at the Laelynn and I need a kit sent down as soon as possible."

A few more words were exchanged before he hung up and put his phone away.

"They're sending everything we need. Don't worry. We're going to figure all of this out."

Another hour and a half passed, during which they searched the remainder of the hotel, looking for any clue as to where he had gone. They came up with nothing, and after assurances from Officer Coello that they would find him, he left.

As her frustration and worry became too much, she went outside and breathed in the fresh air, walking along the gardens out front, using the light from the windows of the hotel to guide her. She walked around the side and was heading towards the back when Luis came around an opposite corner and stopped.

"Luis!" she yelled as she saw him.

He gave her a fearful look and turned to leave.

"Hey!" she screamed, breaking into a run. "I need to talk to you!"

He froze where he was as she approached, his face becoming more fearful.

"Have you seen Alan?" she asked him.

He fumbled with his words, stuttering before finally saying, "No, but I have heard that he's missing."

She felt frustrated. Something in his face told her that he knew more than he was letting on.

"I need to know!" she demanded, her voice on the edge of yelling.

"We've been good to you! We've shown nothing but kindness and we've tried being supportive when you were getting in shit!"

He looked away.

"Now tell me! Where is he?" she screamed.

He kept looking away from her gaze, reminding her of a scared dog that had been disciplined.

"You don't understand," he finally said, his voice quivering with anxiety as his eyes shot around, looking for anyone that might be listening.

"Understand what?" she asked, physically pushing him around the corner to the back of the hotel.

"You don't understand what's happening here," he said, shrinking before her. "This is so much bigger than you."

She grabbed him and shoved him into the wall. "What's going on?" she demanded.

He wrestled her grip away, looked around, and then began speaking.

"This place isn't a resort," he said, "it's a cult, and they've got Alan hidden in there. I saw him earlier. He was beaten up and bleeding badly, but he was alive."

She stood for a moment in silence. She could feel panic setting in. "What do they want?" she asked.

"You," he said. "They don't need Alan for long, but he's going to be the leverage to make sure you cooperate."

"Where is he?" she asked again. "I'm going to get him and we're leaving this place!"

He looked into her eyes. "It's not that easy."

Suddenly, at the front of the hotel, they could hear Hugh and Elena.

"Luis!" Hugh yelled.

After a moment, Elena screamed, "Luis!"

"I have to go!" he said as he started to walk.

"No!" she demanded, shoving him back to where he was.

"If they catch us talking and find out what I've said, they'll take you, and then kill Alan and I tonight!" he said, his voice about to break.

She listened as Hugh and Elena came down the side of the hotel.

"Please," Luis said. "Meet me here at the same time tomorrow and I'll tell you whatever you want to know!"

The footsteps were getting closer.

"Luis!" Elena yelled.

"Please," he pleaded again, cupping his hands in front of himself.

Reena nodded and ducked into a large copse of trees directly behind her. She stood quietly as Hugh and Elena came around the corner.

"We were calling for you!" Elena said as she grabbed him, shoving him in front of her as Hugh took hold of his arm.

"What were you doing back here?" he asked Luis, bending his arm back slightly.

Luis gasped in pain. "I was just checking the area," he said, grimacing.

Hugh laughed and released his arm. "Get going," he said. "We've got more competent people than you to do that!"

Reena walked out from the thick trees and stood on the sidewalk. She wanted to trust Luis, and she hoped she could.

Reena returned to their room and sat on the bed. Immediately, she began to sob. She was hit by a weakness that struck her to her core, and she felt completely powerless. It was a feeling she wasn't used to, and she tried desperately to fight it off.

She pictured her mother and father, arguing across the kitchen table with liquor on their breaths. She pictured her father snorting a line of coke and then rubbing his nose, laughing to himself as he did it.

And then, she pictured Jack and Maria. She thought of her graduation from high school and then from university. She thought of the first meeting with Alan and their engagement, and she thought of the life they had and would return to. Instantly, she felt her inner strength return and she rubbed the tears from her face.

Standing, she walked to the bathroom and looked in the mirror. The red mark from the slap was gone. Her eyes were puffy from crying, but she didn't care. The ring on her finger from Alan shone in the light of the vanity and she rubbed it. She would find her fiancé and they would leave this place together. She knew this, and as she grabbed her purse, removed the gun and sat on the bed, waiting for morning, she felt content with what she had to do.

12

The following day, Reena didn't leave her room except to eat breakfast and lunch. A sense of paranoia began to show, and she had to continually work to supress it. She would be no good if she lost her determined mental state, and she knew it. The hotel was a dangerous place, and she had worked hard the previous night to uncover enough inner strength to do what was needed, even if that meant killing someone.

She thought of Alan and where he was within the hotel. She was worried, but she trusted Luis and was hopeful that he was right when he said Alan was alive.

The time ticked by slowly and she felt herself becoming impatient. The gun had never left her reach. It was either sitting beside her in her room or tucked into her pants while she ate. Its weight gave her a sense of security.

She yawned loudly and rested her head on the pillow. It was only five in the afternoon, and she had another five and a half hours before she was due to meet Luis behind the hotel.

Have a nap, she thought to herself as she watched the muted TV. The images were becoming hypnotic and she felt her eyes becoming heavy.

She rolled over in bed, facing the empty spot that Alan would normally occupy, and breathed in the scent of him that remained. She sighed and grabbed his pillow, holding it close to her and cuddling with it as she fell asleep.

She awoke and looked around the room. It was dark outside and the only source of light was the silent TV.

She looked over at the clock. It was nine. She sat up, tossing Alan's pillow aside, and clicked on her bedside lamp.

The light spread out and illuminated something on the floor by the front door. It was a piece of paper, and as she walked over, picked it up and opened it, she saw that it was a note from Luis.

'I can't meet you at ten thirty. They have Ava, and I'm so scared that they'll hurt her if they catch me. I'll come by your room at three a.m. Please be awake.'

She walked back to the bed and sat down, re-reading the note.

They took his daughter, she thought to herself as she crumpled it up and felt a surge of sympathy for Luis.

She had six hours to wait and she was still tired and starving. She rested her back on the wall, slid her feet into the bed, and clutched the gun in her hands.

At three, there was a soft knock on the door and Reena stood up, quickly walking to it and answering before a second knock sounded.

It was Luis, and in his hands, he held a plastic bag with something in it.

"Come in," she said as she pulled him into the room, checking behind him that he was alone. He handed her the bag and she opened it. It was food.

"I didn't see you downstairs for dinner and I was worried about you," he said as he slid the chair out from the desk and sat down.

She felt touched and sat on the bed to open the container. It was beef soup, and a bun wrapped in a napkin.

"That's sweet of you," she said to him as she started eating the soup. It was cold, but she didn't care.

"They took Ava," he started saying, his voice cracking. "They took my daughter. Hugh called me into his office this morning and told me they had her and my cooperation was necessary or they'd hurt her."

She set the soup aside.

"We'll get her back," she said, looking straight into his eyes. "If we have to kill every one of them, we'll get her and Alan back."

Luis nodded. "I hope so." His face showed worry.

She adjusted her seat on the bed. "I need you to tell me everything you know."

He looked at her for a moment. "Okay," he said softly. "They have Alan and Ava in Hugh's study. It's on the first floor, just behind the office. I saw them with Alan yesterday. He was attacked in the pool room and knocked out. Elena and Hugh dragged him out of the water and when he was conscious enough to walk, they forced him into the study. He's tied up and in pain, but he's alive."

Reena breathed a sigh of relief.

"I don't know why, but they need you," he said, pointing at her. "You're the only one they want."

She watched his face and believed him. "Keep going," she said. "I need to know everything."

He continued. "They're going to force me to bring you to them tomorrow night at ten. You have to come with me or they'll hurt Ava."

He told her about the history surrounding the hotel. He told her about Arthur and Helen, Robert and Charles, and the mysteries surrounding their deaths. He told her about the pit in the back of the property that was still used to discard bodies and mentioned that Lily and John were in the pit as well, and how the bars on the windows were there to keep the guests from escaping.

Reena shook her head sadly.

"That's why Hugh knocked John off the roof," he said, confirming her suspicions that he was purposely knocked off.

"Why did he want to kill him?" she asked.

"Because he was becoming suspicious about the hotel," Luis said, shaking his head. "Hugh was worried that he would figure it out and tell everyone else what was going on. Haven't you noticed that there's no other guests around?"

"Where are they?" she asked cautiously.

"Out back, in the pit."

She paused, thinking of a question. "Where do they kill them?"

"Across the road, there's that small house," Luis said, pointing. "In there. They're superstitious about anyone dying on the property. If John had died where he landed, I think Hugh would have been very upset."

Again, she shook her head.

"I think Maria is back there too," he said, lowering his head at the thought of his wife. "I don't know for sure, but I'm certain she was murdered by Hugh and thrown back there."

He was quiet for a moment and then continued. "Have you noticed the patrols that walk back and forth out front and down to the beach?"

Reena nodded.

"They keep an eye on what goes on around here and report back to Hugh and Elena, who, by the way, are married. Everything here is connected," he said. "Oh, and that police officer that was here? He's not a police officer, he's Elena's brother."

Reena clenched her jaw, feeling the pressure of her teeth grinding on one another.

"They searched your bags, too. They search everyone's bags. When you first arrived here, do you remember leaving your luggage at the front gate, and then they were carried up for you? That's when they searched them."

She laughed to herself, realizing how ludicrous it was.

"I'm worried for my daughter," he said, "but I'm also worried for myself, as selfish as that is."

Reena shook her head. "It's not selfish."

"They flog us, you know. When we don't do what we're supposed to, Hugh calls us into his study and makes us lay across a chair, and then he flogs us until he thinks we've learned a lesson."

"That's why your back was sore that day Alan touched you. You didn't stumble on the stairs, did you?" she asked.

Luis shook his head. "No, I didn't stumble on the stairs. The day before was when I dropped those trays in the dining room, and he punished me for causing a disturbance."

Again, she felt her jaw tightening.

"Do you think we'll get Ava back?" he asked her.

She nodded. "Yes, we will. And Alan too. We'll get them both back."

Luis shrugged. "But how?"

"I have a plan," she said.

"I'll help in anyway I can," he said, reaching towards her and gently touching her hand.

She looked at him, focused, and said, "Oh, don't worry, you're a big part of it."

$$13$$

The next day at noon, Reena went downstairs for lunch. She was tired from the talk with Luis. It had been a lot to take in, and long after he left she lay awake, her thoughts racing.

They had a plan set up to start at nine p.m., and she was anxious for it to take place. The first major step was for her to get the keys to the building. Luis knew that only Hugh and Elena had a set, and without them their plan would fall through. Reena had been watching Elena throughout the morning and early part of the afternoon, waiting for an opportunity. They might notice them missing, but they wouldn't be able to change the locks before Reena was able to act.

Luis would be coming at nine forty-five to get her and take her to Hugh. He would tie her hands and walk her to his study. She knew she had to put faith in him and trust him, but part of her was reminded of the deceit that the entire building carried with it. The people who lived here were dangerous, and as much as she did trust him, he was one of those people. She thought he was different but she didn't know that for sure.

She pushed the thought out of her mind and continued with her day. Elena wasn't predictable with her routines, and at some point, Reena knew she'd have to use force to get the keys.

Throughout the day, Reena was aware that she was being watched. They didn't let her leave their sight, and she had had to push her way through some guards when she decided to take the walk to the beach. She returned a few hours later and couldn't help but wonder what made her so special to them.

At dinner time, she returned to the dining room and picked at her salad. She wasn't hungry and she couldn't keep her eyes off her watch. It was six-thirty, and she could feel a growing sense of anxiety building inside her.

After dinner, she returned to her room and sat on the bed, going through everything in her mind. Several times she had to talk herself down from having a breakdown, and she succeeded in bringing herself back to reality.

As the time turned to eight-thirty, she went to her bedroom door and opened it, peering down the hallway. It was empty. She sighed. Her throat was dry.

"Calm down," she said to herself as she shut the door quietly and walked to the bed.

She picked up the gun and opened the door again, peering down the hallway. Again, it was empty, and she stepped out. The door clicked closed behind her and she nervously made her way towards the stairs.

As she reached the lobby, she stopped and stepped back behind the wall. Elena had walked out from behind the front desk and was making her way to the dining room. As quietly as possible, Reena followed her, using whatever she could to hide herself in case she turned around.

She held her breath as they entered the empty dining room.

Elena went into the kitchen and she followed.

Inside, Elena moved through the fryers and ovens, heading towards a room in the back. Reena held back and let her go into it and shut the door behind her.

After a minute, the door opened. Elena froze in place.

"Back inside!" Reena said, moving closer to Elena. "Sit down!" she said as she shut the door behind her. "If you move, I'll shoot you. If you scream, I'll shoot you."

Elena sat down and dropped some paperwork on the desk. "Now what?" she asked.

"Give me your keys," Reena said, pointing to the desk. "Throw them there."

Elena reached into her pocket and pulled them out. "You won't get out of here," she said as she dropped them.

"Shut up," Reena said, grabbing the keys and turning towards the door. "If you make any noise, I'll come back in here and you will die," she said as she opened it and backed out, keeping her eyes on Elena.

She started to shut the door and find the key when Elena jumped up and ran towards her. She hit the door and it pushed back, surprising Reena, and she stumbled and fell against one of the metal cabinets.

Elena slid forward and onto the tile, but quickly jumped up and grabbed for the knife block.

She screamed as she swung towards Reena, just missing her chest. The knife caught the florescent lighting in its blade and became confusing while Elena swung it, and it connected with Reena's arm. It struck deep, and as Elena pulled it out, a stinging pain shot through her arm.

Reena dove forward as Elena's arm was above her and tackled her to the ground, slamming her head against the tile, stunning her. She grabbed the gun off the floor and ran into the dining room.

Elena quickly followed, panting as she chased after her. They exited the dining room and ran into the lobby, then into one of the hallways.

Reena lost her grip on the gun and watched it bounce off the floor and land by the wall. Misjudging where Elena was, she bent down to pick it up and was thrown into the wall by Elena's body.

Elena screamed as she brought the knife straight down, stabbing into the carpet just as Reena moved her head out of the way. She threw her arm up and then down again, missing another time when Reena quickly moved.

"I'll kill you!" Elena screamed as they wrestled on the floor.

Reena pulled her legs up and kicked hard, throwing her off just enough to pull herself together.

"Come here!" Elena said as she crawled back towards her.

At the end of the hallway, the wall moved. The wallpaper formed a crease as some of the plaster gave way and crumbled. A long, black arm jutted out and down, followed by another. The figure's head was next, and its white eyes shot down the hallway and focused on them as they continued fighting.

Its legs bent in front of it and it slid out of the wall, breaking into a quick crawl as it charged down the hallway.

Reena could see it approaching and began to panic. It's humanoid shape, grotesque and monstrous, struck her with fear. "Stop!" she screamed at Elena. "There's something coming!"

Elena brought the knife down and it stuck in her shoulder. She screamed and reached for it as the figure caught up to them. Its long hand grabbed Elena and threw her a few feet. She landed hard and turned around, her face freezing in fear when she saw what it was.

It crawled to her and stopped when it was above her.

"I'm sorry!" she screamed.

The figure stared at her for a moment and then moved its hands to her head, grasping it on either side.

"I did what you wanted!" she screamed.

The figure didn't speak, gripping her harder.

"Please don't," she begged as it brought one hand over her mouth and the other towards the back of her head.

Her muffled screams could be heard as the figure jolted its hands and her head was violently turned to the side. A cracking sound echoed and Reena turned her eyes away. The figure had broken Elena's neck, and as she looked back at the scene, the figure began crawling to her.

She slid back and hit the wall, then abruptly stood. The figure stood as well, walking directly to her.

She tried to speak but couldn't, and she wondered if it would even understand what she might say.

It came up to her and put both of its hands on either side of her, pausing to stare. She closed her eyes against its white gaze.

After a moment, it stepped forward and through her. She felt a sharp stab of cold in her body and opened her eyes, then turned. A wisp of black mist floated from the wall towards her, and she used her hand to brush it away.

There was nothing left in the hallway except herself and Elena. The figure was gone and the only remnants of it were the broken wall at the other end.

She breathed deeply and looked to Elena. She wanted to feel sorry for her, but she knew that she had it coming.

She waited a few minutes, calming her nerves, before she removed the keys from her pocket and walked to one of the doors. She matched the door number to the key and opened it, then walked back and grabbed Elena's leg. She struggled to pull the body to the door, but slowly she succeeded, dragging it in far enough and then closing the door behind her.

She looked at her watch. It was nine-thirty and Luis would be at her room in fifteen minutes.

She touched her shoulder and noticed that it wasn't hurting. She pulled open her shirt and saw that the stab wound was gone, and then she looked at her arm. That mark was also gone. *Did it heal me?* she wondered.

She ran to the end of the hallway, grabbing the knife, and went into the stairwell. Inside the bedroom, she could feel anticipation building to leave this place and never come back.

Fifteen minutes later, Luis knocked on her door and then opened it with his key card, stepping inside. In his hand he had a pair of handcuffs.

Reena gave him the keys.

"Remember, I'll bang on the door when I have them," she said while he put the keys in his pocket and then put the handcuffs on her.

"The right one isn't closed," he said as he turned her around.

The thought of trusting him rushed through her and she moved her right wrist. She could feel that it wasn't fastened and breathed a sigh of relief.

"When you're done, make sure you come back to the study," she said as they left her room and walked down the hallway to the stairs.

Luis was nervous.

As they approached the study door, Reena could feel her legs turning soft. She was nervous, too, but as the thought of Alan being on the other side of the door came to her, she felt her muscles tighten again.

"Okay," Luis said, shaking badly.

He knocked loudly on the door and waited.

Slowly, the handle turned and Hugh appeared, a big smile spreading across his face.

"Did you search her?" he asked Luis.

"Yes," Luis said, stepping back.

Reena could feel the gun in her waist and the knife that was shoved up her sleeve as Hugh reached over, grabbed her shoulder, and pulled her into the room.

Immediately, she focused on two people sitting against the wall. Alan and Ava. They were both blindfolded, their mouths gagged, their hands and feet bound, but they appeared to be alright. Standing to their side was another employee.

"Alan!" she screamed, trying to break Hugh's grip from her shoulder and run to him.

His head jolted upwards and he tried speaking through the cloth.

"Let go!" Reena said as she jerked her shoulder back and broke Hugh's grip. She ran to Alan and slid down the wall, sitting beside him.

"You can go," Hugh said to Luis as he started closing the door.

After it closed, on the other side, Luis quietly slid the key in the lock and turned it. He stared at the door for a moment and then left.

Inside, Hugh sat at his desk and swiveled on the chair.

"Look," he said as he cleared his throat. "If you cooperate, this will work out much better for you all."

Reena released her right hand from the handcuffs and slid the knife down her wrist, cupping it in her hand.

Beside her, the employee stood.

She stood and swung her hand up and then down, plunging the knife into his neck until its blade disappeared. She pulled it back out. Blood spurted and the man wavered and then fell back, landing on the floor.

Hugh jumped from his chair and ran to the door. He grasped the handle and pulled, but it didn't budge. He tried again, grunting as he did, and then stopped. He turned towards Reena, who was pointing the gun at him.

"Luis," he said.

She nodded and bent towards Alan. She slid off the blindfold and then removed the cloth from his mouth.

"You won't get out of here," Hugh said, releasing the doorknob.

"Oh yes," she said as she moved the knife to Alan's wrists and cut the rope securing them, "we will."

Hugh laughed to himself.

She handed the knife to Alan and he cut the rope on his ankles, then he reached towards Ava to cut her bindings and removed her gag.

"Leave her blindfold on," Reena said as she focused on Hugh.

Alan nodded and whispered in her ear. "Don't worry."

Ava nodded timidly.

"If I had cooperated, they'd already be burning in that pit out back," Reena said.

Hugh hesitated and then nodded.

"And if I had cooperated, I'd never get to leave here."

Hugh shook his head. "That's not true. In a few months you would have been disposed of too."

She felt a shudder move through her body.

"You're not leaving," he said as he moved towards the desk and sat on it. "There's a plan for you. Something is waiting."

She laughed. "That 'something' killed your wife a little while ago."

He frowned. "Elena? She's dead?"

Reena nodded and leaned against the wall.

"He wouldn't do that!" he said, his voice angry.

"He? Whatever it was broke her neck. I heard the crack and saw her empty eyes. She came at me with a knife and that thing killed her," Reena said.

Hugh paused a moment. "She fucked up then," he said, coldly.

"You're going to die too," Reena said as she aimed the gun and then leaned towards Alan.

"Cover her ears," she said to him, nodding towards Ava.

He leaned over and cupped her ears, firmly pressing down.

Hugh stood and took a step towards her. "You won't get out of here!" he yelled, his voice echoing off the walls. "We're all victims of circumstance at some point, and that includes you too!"

Reena stepped forward and squinted her eyes. "We're no one's victims," she said as she pulled the trigger.

A bang sounded and a flash of light from the barrel went through the room as Hugh fell backwards.

Alan released his grip from Ava's ears while Reena banged on the door with her fist.

They heard a click as the lock was released and it opened. Luis was standing on the other side, anxiously looking in.

"You can take off your blindfold, honey," Reena called to Ava.

She did, and looked around cautiously, seeing her father in the doorway. She jumped up and ran to him, desperately hugging him.

He bent down and kissed her and then stood back up. "Everything is done. They're all locked up," he said as he handed the gun and a couple of lighters to Reena.

He had told her the night before that at ten, the employees did a shift change and a briefing of the previous shifts events. They met in one of the rooms in the basement, and all guard posts around the hotel were abandoned for half an hour. The only guard that remained was the one at the front entrance. Tonight, Luis had waited until they were all together and locked them in the room.

She handed him the gun. "You'll need this for the guard at the front," she said.

He took it and held it away from Ava.

"Now go!" Reena said to him.

He hugged her quickly and then picked Ava up. "Thank you!" he said as he took off running towards the exit.

Reena walked to the window and peered out. A moment later, she heard the muffled gun fire and watched the guard at the front fall over.

Luis and Ava ran through the entrance and down the road, disappearing into the night.

Alan and Reena made their way to the basement and into the storage room, grabbing anything they could find that was flammable. They found a few bottles of lighter fluid, a can of paint thinner, and several jerrycans filled with gasoline.

She handed Alan a lighter and picked up the can of paint thinner and the lighter fluid. "Take those and follow me," she said, nodding towards the jerrycans.

He grabbed the cans and followed her into the lobby.

"Leave one of those here," she said, and he set one of them on the ground.

"We're lighting this place on fire and then we're leaving." she said.

They stepped onto the top floor. She opened the can of paint thinner and walked the length of the hallway, spilling it as she went.

"I'm going to go start on the other floors," Alan said as he kicked the door to the stairs open. "Meet me in the lobby when you're done."

She nodded and threw the can to the side, then opened the lighter fluid and took the stairs down a few floors.

She finished and went to their room, quickly grabbing their passports, wallets, and suitcases. She made her way to the lobby and slumped her body on the sofa while she waited for Alan.

She felt a fear growing inside her, an anxious nausea like she might be sick. A pain began in her stomach and radiated out, and all of the energy she had instantly dissipated.

"Okay," Alan said, running into the lobby.

Reena stood and walked to the last can of gasoline.

"What about the people in the basement?" he said, watching as she opened it.

"For what they've all done, they can burn."

He watched as she carried the can to the far corner and slowly began spilling it on the floor. They backed to the entrance as she emptied the can.

She threw the can to the side as they stepped out, reaching into her pocket and removing a lighter and a balled-up piece of fabric.

"Step back," she said as she lit the fabric and threw it into the lobby.

The flames sat for a moment before catching the gasoline on the ground. In one bright flash, the fire spread throughout the floor and ignited the curtains and couch. The front desk was soon engulfed, and the pictures on the walls quickly burst into flames and fell, smashing on the ground.

She slammed the door shut and locked it.

They stepped back and watched as each floor slowly began to light up. After a few minutes, several of the windows burst and flames erupted out.

The hotel was fully engulfed. They could feel the immense heat on their backs as they walked to the road, stopping when a small explosion blew part of the roof off.

They each stood in silence, listening to the splintering of the wood and the roar of the fire before Alan touched her shoulder.

"Let's go," he said, nodding towards Sun Garden. "I want to leave this place."

She nodded and leaned into him as they left.

When they were far enough from the hotel, they turned around and noticed something on the other side of the road. Figures, ghostly and white, began to form and watch the fire. Under a set of obscure trees across from the hotel, two men stood, watching. They recognized one as John, but the other they were unsure of.

On the grounds of the little house just down from the hotel, a mass of figures slowly stepped to the edge of the property and looked at the fire.

"I think they're the people that were murdered," Reena said quietly.

Alan hugged her.

"Let's get out of here," she said.

The next morning, they checked out of their room at one of the hotels in Sun Garden and waited for the bus to arrive. The front desk agent hadn't asked any questions once she found out the Laelynn was burning down, and gladly gave them a room.

They didn't sleep and found themselves watching through their window as the glow from the distant fire lit up the night sky. The hours passed by but the flames never changed.

They cried with one another, feeling a week worth of emotions being released and held each other for the remainder of the night.

A large crowd of bus passengers gathered around them as it pulled up and they stepped on, picking a secluded seat at the back. It pulled away a few moments later and turned onto the road, making its way by the hotel.

As they passed by, they watched through their window. The entire building had collapsed and some parts were still on fire. Smoke rose everywhere, and the odd police officer walked around, pointing to several spots.

When it disappeared from their sight, Reena leaned on Alan's shoulder and thought about their return home. The bus was taking them back to Cancun and they would board a flight within the next few hours to New York.

She rubbed her stomach, feeling a slight ache inside, and her thoughts focused on the idea of moving from the city and starting fresh.

"I love you," she said to Alan, and he kissed her head.

"I love you too."

She smiled and felt her body relax, then she breathed in a sigh of relief and slowly fell asleep.

14

The next day, they awoke in their condo to hear the hustle of the city around them.

"It's good to be home," Reena said as she rolled over in bed and cuddled against Alan.

He nodded and rubbed her back, using his fingertips to tickle her ribs.

She laughed and moved his hand away, reaching up to his forehead and gently rubbing the mark that remained.

"It might scar," she said, using her nursing skills to examine it.

"A reminder of our week together," he laughed.

She smiled. "As if we need a reminder."

They laid in bed for a bit longer until each of their phones rang almost simultaneously.

On his phone, it was his father, and on hers, it was Maria. They had no doubt heard the news about the hotel burning down and were frantically calling to make sure they were okay.

"Yes, we're fine," Reena said to Maria, shouting to be heard as Jack yelled into the receiver with her on the other end. "We're fine!" she yelled, standing and walking to the kitchen so she didn't disturb Alan.

"We're alright, Dad. Don't worry. We got out before it burned down," Alan said to his father.

"They said a group of people died in the basement," his father said, his voice rising with panic.

"Yes, but we weren't those people," Alan said as he stood and walked to the doorway of their bedroom, peering into the kitchen at Reena.

She rolled her eyes and threw a hand in the air, and he made a talking motion with his hand. They both laughed as he disappeared back into the bedroom.

"I'll call you later," he said to his father, trying to usher him off the phone.

"I love you guys," his father said.

"Yes, I love you too and I'll pass your love onto Reena," he said, staring at the wall. "Okay, okay. Yes, that sounds good. Bye, bye." He pulled the phone down and disconnected the call.

Reena walked through the door and grabbed her laptop off their dresser. She opened it and turned it on.

"No one can say we aren't loved," she said, joking as she clicked the internet and searched for the hotel.

"What are you doing?" Alan asked.

"I'm searching to see what it says about the hotel," she said as she clicked.

The main website for the resort was down, with a banner that simply read "Closed".

"Someone updated the site," she said, pointing to the screen. "I wonder if there were others that weren't at the hotel when it burned."

Alan shrugged his shoulders. "There probably was," he said. "We don't know how far it reached."

She closed the browser and then shut the laptop, pausing for a few minutes before she moved it beside her and turned to him. He bent down, kissing her as she tugged on his shirt and pulled him back into bed.

A few weeks after returning home, Reena had started to constantly feel nauseated and wondered if she had contracted a stomach flu. It didn't pass, and she realized that her symptoms were those of pregnancy.

She kept it hidden from Alan until she knew for certain, and one day after work, she bought a pregnancy test.

The minutes seem to pass by slowly, and when she finally looked she felt a shock spread through her. It was positive. She felt happy, but nervous as well. A week later she saw a doctor and it was confirmed that she was about two to three weeks pregnant.

"Do you remember how I thought I had the flu?" she asked.

He nodded, not looking up from the computer. "You went to the doctor and he gave you something for it."

"Well, yes. I went to the doctor, but it's not the flu."

He looked at her. "What was it?"

She held up the pregnancy test. "It was this."

He stood up, walked to her, and grabbed the test from her. "This is so exciting!" he said, rubbing her stomach.

"There's nothing in there yet," she said, swatting his hand away. "It's just a bit of yeast and some flour so far."

He laughed and continued rubbing her stomach. She could see how happy the news made him.

"I think we should leave the city," she said, laying her hand on top of his.

He nodded. "Wherever you want to go is good with me," he said.

She was surprised that he immediately agreed, but thankful that he didn't protest. He could move his business wherever they went, and she could look for a new nursing job. Within a week, they had listed their condo and began actively searching for another place to move.

She had mentioned their intent to move to colleagues, and she was soon offered a transfer to a hospital in Stowe, Vermont. Alan looked into moving his business and they found that it was possible. They could pick up their life, exactly how it was, and place it in the small town, allowing themselves to enjoy life a little bit more.

A month later, they had an offer on their condo. It didn't leave a lot of room for profit, but it was a small sacrifice for the excitement of their new life.

Soon after, their condo was packed and the movers were loading the truck. It felt bittersweet to leave their first home, but it quickly faded to excitement.

In no time, their new house was unpacked and set up.

Reena had started to show her pregnancy and feel the pains of it shortly after settling. It peaked during her third trimester, and she was forced to take a leave from work and remain at home, doing as little as possible to ease any danger to herself or the baby.

They had decided to keep the gender a secret until it was born, and as the final weeks stretched on, they made a list of baby names they liked.

"I like Amelia," Alan suggested as he read from a baby name book.

"I do too. What about Lucas?" she asked, flipping through the second book they had.

"I like it," he said.

They had received a small gift from Luis and Ava after they reconnected online. He had made his way back home to Cancun after fleeing the hotel and was living with his brother.

Alan and Reena were happy to hear that he had been able to get to safety, and they kept in touch over the months through weekly emails and phone calls. He was elated for them when he found out they were expecting and sent them a baby blanket and a card expressing his well wishes. Inside was a picture of himself and Ava.

"It's so sweet," Reena said, sticking it to the fridge.

"It is," Alan said as he stood beside her, looking at it.

In the middle of the night, Reena awoke to pains in her stomach and wet bed sheets.

"Wake up!" she yelled, violently shaking Alan.

He turned and faced her, rubbing his eyes. "What's wrong?"

She had slid her feet to the side of the bed and sat up. "My water broke!"

Panic flooded the room and he jumped up and ran to her side, mumbling to himself as he fumbled with her slippers.

She groaned in pain and kept grabbing at her stomach.

"Don't let it out yet," he said, quickly putting his pants and shirt on. He ran back to her and helped her stand up.

The hospital was only a couple of blocks away, and as he pulled up and ran to her side of the car, she screamed again, grabbing the seat in pain.

They burst into the emergency room and he sat her on a chair, then ran to the front desk and began yelling at the attendant in panic.

"My wife is having a baby! She's having it right now!"

The woman behind the desk calmly picked up the phone as she

shut the privacy glass in front of her. She spoke to someone for a moment and then hung up. Soon after, a few nurses and a doctor came into the waiting room and whisked Reena away.

Three hours later, the baby was born. It was a boy, and they welcomed it together.

"Lucas," she said, staring at him with both admiration and fear.

"We're parents," Alan said, feeling the weight of the words.

There was a moment of silence, and then one of the nurses spoke. "Yes, you are, and your life is now over for eighteen years." She laughed loudly to herself and disappeared around a corner as Alan and Reena looked at one another and felt joy.

The next few weeks were a blur of baby showers and visits from friends and family. Jack and Maria stayed for a week, and Alan's father stayed for two. Their house had become the go-to for everyone, and as much as they enjoyed all their guests and the help they offered, they wanted time to settle down and enjoy Lucas to themselves.

When the last guest left and they waved goodbye, they both let out a sigh of relief as Lucas squirmed in Reena's arms.

"He doesn't cry," she said as she held him up.

"That's why he's the best baby," Alan said, putting his arm around her.

He hadn't cried once since they brought him home, and as they recalled, he hadn't even cried when he was born. Their expectation was for him to always be screaming, as most newborns did, but they were happily surprised by how quiet he was.

The sun set slowly as they tucked him into his crib, covering him and arranging the teddy bears in a circle around him.

"Is it what you thought it would be?" Reena said as she tugged the curtains over the window and darkened the room.

Alan nodded. "It is," he said, standing back and watching Lucas sleep soundly.

They exited the room and shut the door quietly, walking down the hallway and to the living room.

Laying on the couch, Alan turned on the TV and lifted his arm. Reena laid beside him and they cuddled one another.

Down the hallway, Lucas stirred and moved the blankets down. A small groan escaped his mouth and his eyes shifted behind his eyelids. They shot open, staring towards the ceiling in a vacant stare.

They were pure white with no pupils. The room dropped in temperature and a deep chill caused his breath to turn into fog. He breathed steadily, keeping his eyes focused above him; never blinking and never moving.

EPILOGUE

"Welcome to The Laelynn," Luis said pleasantly, welcoming the guests. "Please, follow me. You can leave your bags here and our hotel staff will be pleased to take them to your rooms...please, follow me."

Alan and Reena followed as everyone walked up the stairs. Behind them, a group of hotel employees carefully picked up their luggage and started carrying them towards the back of the hotel. They took them into a private room.

Hugh stepped in front of a table and opened the luggage placed on top.

"We need to make this quick," he instructed the other employees, and began looking through all the belongings in the bag.

He removed a box of condoms from the suitcase and placed it beside him, then reached into his pocket and pulled out a long needle. He opened the box and pulled out the condoms, then began poking all of them, ensuring there were multiple holes in each.

After damaging them, he finished looking through the suitcase and shut it, zipping it closed as he read the nametag: Alan Trino.

He moved to another suitcase on the table and opened it. After flipping through its contents and finding nothing, he shut it. The nametag flipped over: Reena Trino.

"Okay," he said, his voice loud over the noise from the other employees. "Finish up quickly and get these bags to the rooms."

He walked to the front desk and saw Luis taking two guests down one of the hallways.

"They're just finishing up," he said to Elena as he approached her.

"Do you think it'll work?" she asked him, staring into the empty lobby.

"Who are we to question him? He said he'd come back from death, and he did. If he wants us to ensure someone can get pregnant while they're here, we need to do it."

She shifted on her feet. "Yes," she said, sounding skeptical. "But a vessel?"

Hugh looked at her disapprovingly. "It's what he believes, and I have faith in him."

She shook her head, stopping abruptly as he grabbed her hand and twisted it.

"Enough of your doubt. He's here, in this hotel. He'll get out eventually," he said.

He let her hand go and she pulled it to back, rubbing it.

She slowly nodded, feeling a chill rise up behind her. They turned and looked down the length of the desk. The black figure stood, quietly watching them. It stared at them for a minute, and then without warning, began to vaporize into the floor and disappeared.

A tap on the counter broke their concentration and they turned to see another set of guests.

Elena smiled widely. "Welcome to the Laelynn."

ABOUT THE AUTHOR

I'm an aspiring author, and writing has always been a secret passion of mine. I've always loved living a vicarious life through the character that I've written, and it is easily one of the most rewarding aspects of creating. I have an imagination that won't quit, and through writing, I've been able to express it and allow it to carry on a life of its own. In the past, I've use painting, drawing, and photography as a means of artistic expression, but writing has always been something that allows unobstructed creativity to flow.
I'm an avid reader, and I believe that's important. It allows us, the readers and writers, to open our minds to other worlds that, if written well, become something believable and inspiring.
I hope that what I write and that my literary path is something that you can join me in.

I want to thank you for reading this book, and I hope that you enjoyed it. I loved writing it.